T3-BPL-279

"You make a lot of assumptions, don't you?" Miranda said.

"It's known as poetic license." He poised himself above her, and his mouth came down with hard, driving force on hers. His hand smoothed its way up her leg, and she stretched out under him like a cat, letting the ripples of longing that his caress created flow through her.

Then, suddenly, his hand was no longer there. His lips slowly left hers, and he sat up. His face, moody and unhappy, was turned to the fire.

"Much as I want you, *macushla*, and it's killing me to want you the way I do, I'll wait until I have your love." He got up abruptly. "And so help me God, Miranda, you're the only woman I've ever felt that way about."

Dear Reader:

Spring is here! And we've got six new SECOND CHANCE AT LOVE romances to add to your pleasure in the new season. So sit back, put your feet up, and enjoy . . .

You've also got a lot to look forward to in the months ahead—delightful romances from exciting new writers, as well as fabulous stories from your tried-and-true favorites. You know you can rely on SECOND CHANCE AT LOVE to provide the kind of satisfying romantic entertainment you expect.

We continue to receive and enjoy your letters—so please keep them coming! Remember: Your thoughts and feelings about SECOND CHANCE AT LOVE books are what enable us to publish the kind of romances you not only enjoy reading once, but also keep in a special place and read again and again.

Warm wishes for a beautiful spring,

Ellen Edwards

Ellen Edwards
SECOND CHANCE AT LOVE
The Berkley Publishing Group
200 Madison Avenue
New York, N.Y. 10016

Second Chance at Love

SPELLBOUND

KATE NEVINS

**SECOND CHANCE AT LOVE
BOOK**

Other Second Chance at Love books by
Kate Nevins

FORBIDDEN RAPTURE   #90
MIDSUMMER MAGIC   #162

SPELLBOUND

Copyright © 1984 by Kate Nevins

All rights reserved. No part of this publication may be reproduced or
transmitted in any form or by any means, electronic or mechanical,
including photocopy, recording, or any information storage and re-
trieval system, without permission in writing from the publisher.

Requests for permission to make copies of any part of the work should
be mailed to: Permissions, Second Chance at Love, The Berkley Publishing Group, 200 Madison Avenue, New York, NY 10016.

First edition published May 1984

First printing

"Second Chance at Love" and the butterfly emblem are trademarks
belonging to Jove Publications, Inc.

Printed in the United States of America

Second Chance at Love books are published by
The Berkley Publishing Group
200 Madison Avenue, New York, NY 10016

Chapter One

HER HAND STILL on the door she had just opened, Miranda paused and surveyed the research laboratory before her affectionately. Wherever she went, she reflected, this organized clutter of microscopes, test tubes, petri dishes, assorted apparatus, and half-drunk mugs of coffee would always be *home*. She'd had several such "homes"; her present one belonged to the Irish branch of Biochem Laboratories in the Killarney district. The lab was empty now; a whimsical OUT TO LUNCH sign hanging from the arm of a microscope told why.

Miranda took the foil-wrapped half of a cheese sandwich from the pocket of her lab coat and put it in the refrigerator. She'd finish eating later; right now she was too excited about the experiment she was doing to care about food.

She went to her workbench, noting with pleasure that Jill, the animal technician, had put the cage of lab mice Miranda had asked for on the Formica counter. She filled

1

a hypodermic syringe with a premixed solution and took one of the mice from the cage. As she held it firmly with one hand and poised the other for the injection, a voice at her elbow made her jump.

"Sure you're not going to plunge that wicked long needle into that poor wee creature, are you now?"

The mouse slithered through Miranda's fingers. She clapped her hand over it, and the needle clattered out of her other hand onto the smooth counter. With a stab of apprehension—why hadn't she heard the door open and what was wrong with security?—Miranda whirled around to face the intruder.

She looked up into eyes that were blue-black under dark lashes and bright with laughter. A straight nose, a long upper lip over a firm mouth, and a squarely carved chin with a deep cleft in the center—Miranda took in these features with the decisiveness of a trained scientific observer. Lunatics, terrorists, and rapists didn't have laugh wrinkles around their eyes and lips that curved upward at the corners. Miranda's fear metamorphosed into annoyance. Strangers were not allowed in the labs. What was this tall, burly Irishman dressed in rumpled green tweeds and a flyaway Christmas-red necktie doing here?

"I'm Dr. Dunn," Miranda said icily. She never used her title, which went with a Ph.D. in biology; but given the respect medical doctors got, if this intruder thought her one, so much the better. She had to do something to ward off the predatory look in those clear blue eyes and wipe that approving smile off his lips.

For a moment, Miranda considered buttoning her lab coat over the curves-clinging knit she had worn against Killarney's autumn damp, but decided that would be demeaning. She had a right to her woman's body, and if a wholesome diet, exercise, and good genes resulted in dimensions that turned male heads, so be it. The flattery was morale-building and didn't affect her work at all—except at the present moment. "Who, if I may ask," she therefore continued sarcastically, "are you?"

The azure eyes opened wide in feigned astonishment. "A doctor! Fancy a mere slip of a girl like you, with hair as yellow as a field of buttercups and eyes..."

Miranda didn't wait for the rest. The space between her hand and the Formica had suddenly become empty. "My mouse! It's gone."

His eyes danced with amusement. "This is Ireland," he said soothingly. "You can always get another."

"No, I can't," she retorted as she looked along the counter, in the stainless steel sink, and then up at the shelves of Erlenmeyer flasks and variously shaped bottles.

"Is it a breed that left the country with the snakes, then?" he asked with sly humor.

"It's not the same kind of mouse," Miranda explained, moving off to search the other counters and sinks. "These are bred for genetic traits under controlled conditions."

"Sounds like a royal wedding night," he murmured.

Miranda laughed. "They're bred at a place in the States. This one is a BALB/c. The letters indicate their heredity."

He had caught up with her now and laid his finger on the lapel of her starched white coat. "You're much nicer when you forget about this."

She took his hand and coolly removed it. Briefly, she noticed the discrepancy between the long, slender fingers and the work-hardened palm. "And *you're* nicer now that you've dropped that stage Irishman act. Trinity College?" she asked, naming Ireland's foremost university. She had been in the country six months, long enough to recognize his accent as a combination of university-educated speech and County Kerry lilt.

Before he could answer, she caught a flash of movement under a far counter. "My mouse!" she screamed. She raced and pounced but missed the animal by a tail's

length and ended up sitting on the floor, her shapely legs
sprawled in front of her.

With two long steps, he was there, shifting around
the supplies cartons on the floor. "I've got him trapped,"
he boasted.

Miranda looked up at him dubiously. "I don't think
so."

"Then perhaps it's you I've got trapped," he said
softly.

"Hardly!" Miranda retorted. She jumped to her feet
and stood for a moment, knowing she should move
away—they were standing too close for strangers—but
unwilling to back down before the challenge in his eyes.
There was a hint of sardonic amusement in their blue
depths and in the slight lift of his finely curved lips. To
some men, the white lab coat was like the matador's red
cape to a bull. They wanted to test the woman who wore
it.

Miranda shrugged and glanced away. Stare-downs
were childish, and she had work to do. She would find
out what this handsome Irishman wanted and send him
on his way. One of the technicians could catch the run-
away mouse. She raised her foot to step over the boxes
ringing her in when a sudden lunge of the stranger's hand
made her jump back.

"I've got him!" he shouted triumphantly, but in grabbing for the mouse he tripped over a box and toppled
both himself and Miranda backward onto the floor.

Startled, Miranda found herself pinned down under
the stranger while his hand reached past her and returned
with a beady-eyed mouse in its grasp. "It's mine!" Miranda yelled, obeying some atavistic instinct of owner-
ship.

"I wasn't going to keep it," he said with a chuckle.

With that, he deftly dropped the mouse into her lab-
coat pocket and held his hand over the flap. She could

feel the warmth of his hand on her side. He looked down at her with an unfathomable expression in his blue eyes. Because of the ridiculous way they were sprawled on the floor, even their legs were entangled. Miranda extricated herself to a sitting position and put her hand over his to remove it from her hip. "I can take care of the mouse now," she said lightly.

"But I feel responsible," he objected, managing with his long, supple fingers both to grasp her hand and hold the flap closed. "You and that BALB/b in your pocket are guests in my country."

"BALB/c," she corrected without thinking. She couldn't think; she was all sensation now. Everywhere he touched her—her hip, which knew the size of his hand; her cheek, fanned by his breath; and her firm, high breasts, flowering under his caressing look—felt deliciously, newly alive.

"Ah, that makes a difference," he said. "I wouldn't want to be kissing a woman who went in for BALB/b mice." Gently, he pressed her to the floor, and Miranda's eyes widened in amazement. She was going to be kissed by a total stranger, with a lab mouse in her pocket! Torpid now, the poor thing was probably as stunned as she was. Was her mouth falling open with the surprise of it all or were her lips parting in soft acquiescence? Evidently, the stranger assumed the latter, because the last thing Miranda saw was an amused, knowing gleam in his eyes.

His lips against hers were cool and firm. The taste of them mingled with his clean, outdoors masculine smell. Moreover, he was experienced and confident, and Miranda liked that. But even as she was finding the kiss a little silly but very pleasant, alarming thoughts kaleidoscoped through her mind. What if someone came in and saw her, staff biologist Miranda Dunn, on the floor being kissed? Who *was* he, anyway? And what had gotten into *her*, to go along with this foolishness?

Then the stark, racking hunger she had almost forgotten about took hold, and the gentle clinging of her mouth gave way to a fierce intensity. Instantly, his kiss conformed to hers. His lips became ravaging pursuers of their own pleasure. They ground hard against hers, satisfying and tantalizing her at the same time.

His hand slipped under her lab coat and around her slim waist, grazing her breast and leaving a wave of sensuous arousal in its wake. A hot, sweet ripening had just started deep within her when there was a sudden scurry over her hip. "The mouse!" Miranda screamed. She clapped her hand across the pocket of her lab coat and scrambled to her feet.

They were both upright now, facing each other. Miranda fought for control, for long, deep breaths and a slowing of the rapid beat of her heart. She was embarrassed but not ashamed. After all, who knew better than a biologist the dictates of the body? And although *he* had no way of knowing it, she *had* been divorced and celibate for a year. Then, brown eyes half narrowed, she studied him closely. Like many women, she had dated heavily after her divorce—as a cure for unaccustomed loneliness, to stave off feelings of rejection, and for a new self-definition vis-à-vis men. And although she had limited her friendships after a while, she had continued dating. But no one had made her feel the way this big Irishman with blue-black eyes did—deliciously tingly all over, as though she had champagne in her veins. Which was all the more reason he had to leave. Brief encounters with strangers were not Miranda Dunn's style.

"You'll have to go," she said in an even-toned, authoritative voice. "In the absence of the department chief, I'm in charge of the lab, and since you don't seem to have any legitimate reason to be here, I'm asking you to leave—right away."

His eyes bright with amusement, he replied, "When

the cat's away, the mice will play. Is that it?"

"More like, the mouse will get squashed," Miranda said wryly, taking the animal from her pocket and returning it to its cage. Over her shoulder, she called out, "The door's there, mister."

He caught up with her and stood watching her maneuvers with the cage. "I have an appointment with Dr. Royce," he said quietly.

Miranda frowned. Something about him didn't bespeak the scientist. It wasn't the comfortable-looking old tweeds or the thick dark hair that looped and curled around his ears and made tiny *u*'s on the nape of his neck. Suddenly, unexpectedly, Miranda wondered how many women had run their fingers through that unruly mane. Then, with stern self-control, she hauled her truant thoughts in and decided she didn't understand how she knew he wasn't a scientist; she just knew.

"The name's O'Bannon," he said lightly. "Brian O'Bannon." He waited, as though for some sign of recognition. As she continued to stare vacantly at him, he smiled. "The poet," he added with an air of self-mockery.

Confusion, disappointment, and even disbelief raced through her mind. Poets didn't have broad shoulders and an easy way about them and fresh, outdoors complexions, did they? They were intense and emotional and pale. Miranda stopped herself. What was wrong with her, going on about poets in that way? Scientists didn't stereotype people; they were too rational for that.

Unable to think of anything to say, Miranda simply repeated, "A poet," and wondered if, given her new stupidity, she couldn't be replaced by a robot that very day.

He was looking at her again in that teasing way he had, his eyes half closed, the blue almost hidden by his dark lashes. "Right," he said, drawing out the *r* while his gaze shifted to her sensuous, full lower lip, "and when properly inspired, I write love poetry."

Miranda moved away and said briskly, "I'm afraid *I* can't depend on inspiration. I have to go to work right now. Dr. Royce's office adjoins the lab." She gestured toward the appropriate door. "The department secretary occupies the office just in front of his. You might be more comfortable waiting there till Dr. Royce returns from lunch. He shouldn't be long."

Ignoring her chatter, O'Bannon said, "I don't know your first name."

"It's Miranda."

"From the Latin, meaning 'to be admired.'"

She laughed shortly. "My father had dreams of glory for me."

A hubbub of conversation announced the return of lab techs, secretaries, and research personnel. "That dark-haired beauty in a hurry is Sheila, Dr. Royce's secretary. He must be back or she wouldn't be." Miranda nodded to the poet then and said pleasantly, "Good-bye, Mr. O'Bannon."

He shook his head. "Not good-bye, Miranda, but *slan is beannacht.*"

"Meaning?" she asked warily.

"Meaning, 'I'll be seeing you.'" His dark blue eyes held hers. "That's a promise, *macushla,*" he said softly.

A short time later, Sheila appeared at Miranda's elbow as she was explaining a procedure to the head lab technician. Sheila was new at the job of research secretary, and according to many people in the department was the fastest typist of misspelled words in Ireland. She had been given a medical dictionary; but as she logically pointed out in a lilting brogue, how could she be expected to find the words she was looking for if she couldn't spell them in the first place? So Sheila had gotten into the habit of coming to Miranda—because "Miss Dunn wasn't stuck-up and laudydaw like some of the others"—

and standing patiently, a sheet of yellow paper covered with the crabbed writing of one of the scientists in her hand, until Miranda could help her. And so it was today.

"What would this hen-scratching be, do you think, Miss Dunn?" Sheila asked, jabbing a pink-tipped finger at a word.

"Immunoelectrophoresis," Miranda said after a quick look.

Sheila frowned at the yellow paper. "And how would you be spelling it?"

Miranda repressed a smile and spelled the word slowly as Sheila wrote it down.

"Thanks, Miss Dunn. I'm a good speller, but these aren't English words at all."

Miranda laughed outright. "Most of them come from Latin or Greek."

"Well, they should have stayed there," the young woman muttered.

As the secretary turned to go, Miranda said, "Sheila?"

"Yes?" Sheila asked, turning back.

Miranda hesitated. Since she had watched that broad tweed-clad back disappear through Dr. Royce's door, she had been unable to get Brian O'Bannon out of her mind. She had found herself smiling and putting her hand over her lab-coat pocket. In the middle of entering data in her lab notebook, she had run her fingers lightly over her mouth, wondering if it had felt soft and sweet to him. Most of all, she was burning with curiosity to know what the name he had called her meant. But did she really want to go on with this silliness about, of all people, a poet? So in answer to Sheila, Miranda shook her head and said, "Nothing," then waved her hand vaguely and added, "Just something I was thinking of."

Sheila smiled, an absent look in her blue eyes. "I have to go," she said with a nod in the direction of Dr. Royce's office. "Himself will be looking for me."

Suddenly contrite, Miranda said, "Oh, I'm so sorry. I didn't mean to keep you. I just wanted to know . . . that is, it's not important . . . but what does *macushla* mean?"

"*Macushla!*" Sheila said with emphasis, her pert face breaking into a broad grin. "What do you want to know that for?"

"I read it somewhere—in an Irish book, I think."

"Then it must have been a love story. *Macushla* means 'darling.' It's a soft, lovely word, isn't it?"

Miranda looked at the secretary in surprise. She hadn't thought of the sound of the word, only its meaning. When Sheila left, Miranda rolled it around on her tongue. *Macushla*. Sheila had been right. It *was* a soft, lovely word. With an absurd bump of her heart, Miranda recalled the longing way Brian had looked at her when he said it and how tender he'd made the word sound.

Later, Miranda remembered that she had forgotten to ask Sheila her other question. Why was the head of Biochem's research department meeting with an Irish poet?

She didn't see O'Bannon leave, possibly because she made it a point to find things to do that took her out of the lab, or more likely because he left Dr. Royce's office by the door that opened out into the hall, the door he should have entered by. But at the end of the day, when Sheila came into the lab again to remind Miranda of her appointment with Dr. Royce, Miranda left her workbench eagerly. Now she'd find out what Brian O'Bannon's business with Biochem Laboratories was.

However, Miranda forgot about the poet momentarily when she walked into Walter Royce's office and spotted its new occupant, a huge reddish-gold salmon, mounted and framed in oak. Royce was an avid fisherman, and Miranda wondered from time to time if it was medical research or the superb fishing possibilities in the many lakes and rivers that had brought him to Ireland.

His eyes following hers, Royce said, laughing, "You should see the one that got away."

"I can't believe it. It must be the biggest salmon ever caught anywhere." Royce beamed; but although she tried to hide it, a slightly puzzled look crept into Miranda's expression. *Did* one display fishing trophies in a scientific office?

Catching her reaction, Royce said sheepishly, "Janet wouldn't let me hang it in the house. It clashes with her antiques."

Miranda smiled. It was an open secret among the closely knit staff that with her children grown and gone, Janet Royce bossily mothered everyone around, including her husband, the prestigious scientist. But Miranda had known about Janet's gentle despotism even before she came to work for Biochem, because the Royces were family friends. Miranda's father and Walter Royce had been classmates at medical school. They had both chosen research instead of a practice, and from time to time through the years they had been on the faculty of the same medical school or had held positions at the same research institute. Curling a finger around a strand of her thick blond hair, Miranda tried unsuccessfully to imagine Dr. Frazier Dunn not being allowed to hang a salmon on the wall of his own home—or anywhere else he wanted.

"How's the experiment going, Miranda?" Royce asked.

"Fine. I think we're going to get some interesting results from that last culture."

Royce nodded. "Good. I wanted to discuss some of your findings to date." He riffled through the papers that blanketed his desk. "Here's your report—suppose we go over it together. Draw up a chair."

Almost an hour later, Royce placed his hand on top of the manila folder and said, "Excellent work, Miranda. Frazier would be proud of you."

"I hope so," Miranda answered simply.

Royce shot her a keen glance from under tufted reddish-gray brows. "He's coming to Killarney at some point, isn't he?"

Miranda nodded. "On his way to Geneva for that international symposium on cell structure."

Standing up, Royce said with a smile, "We'll have to entertain him in grand style. I'll take him fishing. Janet will want to cook a gourmet dinner, I'm sure. We'll show him around the lab"—his smile broadened— "maybe even subject him to a poetry reading."

"A poetry reading?" Miranda couldn't help echoing, but she managed to avoid a note of incredulity.

Royce's smile widened into a whole sunbeam. "If you'll excuse the expression, I've hooked an Irish poet for Biochem's 'Evening with the Arts,'" he explained complacently. "He's well-known, so you may have heard of him. His name's Brian O'Bannon."

"I've heard of him," Miranda said dryly. "But why in the world did you want a poet for the program?"

Royce shrugged. "Why not? We've had a flautist and a concert singer. The committee left it up to me, and I thought we should do something different, something not in the musical line."

"I know, but poetry!" Miranda made a face.

Royce looked surprised. "What have you got against poetry?" His voice became stern. "If you have strong opinions or reservations about possible programs, you should participate more, Miranda. We could use you on the committee. But before you object to anything, just remember those long, boring nights before we started this cultural program, when there wasn't anything to do but watch TV or go to a singing pub in Killarney."

"I stand rebuked, sir," Miranda said with a laugh. "It might even do me some good to hear a little poetry—a very little."

To her surprise, he didn't come back with a laugh. "It very well might," he said seriously. "Sometimes we forget that there are other things in life besides science."

Miranda looked steadily at him. "You know, I don't believe that," she said lightly. "Oh, I don't mean that I don't believe life is a many-faceted affair. Of course it is. But I don't believe in dilettantism. I *want* to pour all of myself into only one pursuit, and that one pursuit is science."

The expression on Royce's face as he studied her was thoughtful and kind, but Miranda wondered if there weren't also a hint of sadness in it. "You're your father's daughter, Miranda," he said at last.

Miranda laughed, a little wryly. "What else? You know how it was in our home—junior chemistry sets for my birthday; a copy of *Microbe Hunters* as a reward for a good report card. I was preparing slides for my own little microscope and dissecting dead frogs when other girls were playing with dolls."

Walter Royce chuckled. "I remember how excited Frazier was when you won first place in the state science fair. He came to me and said, 'The girl has an aptitude for science,' and there was something like awe in his voice."

"Science is Dad's lodestar in the disorderly, irrational world of human beings," Miranda replied with amused resignation. "I thought he'd be pleased when I married a scientist, but he wasn't. Maybe he knew Craig and I wouldn't make a go of it."

"I still think you two didn't try hard enough," Royce said reprovingly.

"Oh, but we did. We just weren't made for a commuter marriage. All that traveling between Minneapolis and New York every weekend or so wore us down. Then there were the weeks when we didn't see each other at all. We might have been able to swing it later on, but as newlyweds . . . " Miranda let her voice trail off. Even an old family friend didn't have to hear everything.

"With the professional promise you both showed, one of you could have gotten a job in the other's city."

"I was ready to do that to save our marriage when it was obvious the arrangement wasn't working out. Given Craig's pride, it would have meant my going to him; but Dad talked me out of it. He said that I was the better scientist, that the move would interrupt my career, and that I might never be able to recoup the lost ground."

"And you listened to him?" Royce sounded shocked.

"It wouldn't have made any difference. The marriage was already dying of attrition." With a grim smile, she added, "Neither of us really cared to make the weekend trip anymore. Also, I found out later that by then Craig was interested in someone else." Miranda moved toward the door. "I feel bad about the collapse of our marriage, but not guilty. Craig remarried recently—she isn't a scientist, by the way—and we're still friends."

"Then why feel bad?"

"Craig and I started out loving each other; it's a shame it couldn't have continued," she said wistfully. Then she looked squarely at the older man. "A failure's a failure no matter what one tries to call it or where it occurs, isn't it?"

"You'll meet someone else," he said comfortingly.

Miranda laughed. "I've met hundreds, all in white lab coats with a breast pocket full of ball-point pens."

Walter Royce smiled. "Just stay out of the darkroom, Miranda. Some of these young fellows are interested in developing more than film."

She smiled back at him as she opened the door. "Tell Janet hello." Miranda was always careful to call her department head by his title, but she treated his wife with an informality that went back to the days when Janet Royce was "Auntie Janet" to the child Miranda.

When Miranda returned to the lab, her raincoat was the last on the coat rack. The fine, persistent rain that penciled Dr. Royce's window, the only one in the lab section, had been going on for days. This was unusual in Killarney, where it rained frequently, but generally only for short periods of time.

As she buttoned her coat and belted it, then squashed a matching rain hat over her smooth, thick hair, Miranda thought of Brian O'Bannon and the astonishing news that he would be reading his poetry at Biochem only a few days hence. Walter had seemed pleased that O'Bannon had agreed to do it so soon. In fact, judging by the expression on her chief's face and the things he had said, Brian O'Bannon was almost as highly esteemed in that office as the golden salmon on the wall.

Miranda stepped out the rear door of the building and stopped. A morass of grayish-brown mud, the consistency of glue, lay between her and the Biochem parking lot. A cement mixer, abandoned at the edge of the asphalt, was evidence that the company was trying to pave the area; but, Miranda surmised, the recent steady rain coupled with some mystery of the soil had delayed completion. Planks had been laid end to end across the field, but they had been trod on so often as to be half submerged in the mud. They looked both slippery and unsteady; and although there would be no danger in sliding off—it was only a field, not a bog—one would come out of it an awful mess.

With a view to using the front door and its paved walk, even though it was farther to the parking lot, Miranda turned the door handle behind her. But the door locked automatically, and she didn't have a key. There was nothing for it but to "walk the plank."

She put one foot gingerly in front of her and brought the other alongside it. The plank was wide enough; it was just the infernal mud that made it so slippery. But the only way through was straight ahead, and Miranda took another small, careful step. Confident now that she had gotten the hang of it, she went slightly faster. Then her foot slid on the mud-slick plank. Instinctively, she reached forward for something to grab on to, and touched thin air. Quickly throwing both arms out to her sides in an effort to regain her balance, she teetered precariously. At that moment, she felt two strong hands on her hips anchor her to the wooden plank.

"Steady, *macushla*," a familiar voice said.

"Where did you come from?" Since she hadn't seen him approach, Miranda had the sudden, absurd vision of his having dropped out of the dark clouds overhead.

"I was using Biochem's library for a little project I have in mind. You didn't hear me when I opened the door because you were concentrating so hard on keeping your balance. Don't talk now. Make your body light as a feather, like a dancer's. Think of it that way. And remember, you're as sure-footed as a Mohawk brave building one of your Manhattan skyscrapers. I'll be doing the same behind you."

Step by step, Miranda moved forward through the curtain of rain, with Brian following, his hands loose but controlling on her sides. She didn't see herself in a tutu, or hawk-eyed and hard-hatted miles above Madison Avenue. Instead, her mouth had gone strangely, unaccountably dry and there was a commotion going on under her ribs that was simultaneously painful and deliciously exciting. She could think of nothing but his closeness to her and the spread of his hands on her hips.

They were midway across the field now and had reached the end of the first plank. Miranda took a long step onto the second one and watched aghast as her foot slid forward and she started to go with it. She felt Brian's hands tighten, heard his, "steady, *macushla*," and thought resentfully, why does he make my heart do absurd somersaults with that silly endearment?

But somehow he kept her upright until she had regained her balance. When they reached the asphalt parking lot, she turned and looked at him. He had bicycle clips on his trousers and was wearing a black rain cape over his tweed jacket, with a rain hood tied under his chin with a much-knotted cord. His face was streaked with rain. It beaded his dark brows and thick lashes. A strand of black hair hung lank and wet on his forehead.

Yielding to a playful impulse, Miranda leaned forward, took the lock of hair between her thumb and index finger, and curled it into a big *C*. With the rain bucketing down over the two of them, she laughed and said, "There, now you have a spit curl."

"In Ireland we call them kiss curls."

Miranda wrinkled her nose. "I don't think it's the same thing."

"It's the same part of the anatomy," he murmured. He pulled her toward him, his lips pressing hers in a long kiss. Wet as they both were she felt as though they were drinking some life-giving elixir from each other. When Brian finally lifted his mouth from hers, her face remained upturned, as she responded to the thrilling beat of a slow, insistent rhythm within her. Placing his hand lightly but masterfully under her jaw, he looked down at her.

"Your eyes are so dark, I can't even see the pupils. They're like the brown in wet pansies." He moved his hand up along her face and under her rain hat. "And your hair is so blond," he continued in a wondering tone. "It's a rare and lovely combination."

Miranda moved away. "Practicing for your poetry reading, Mr. O'Bannon?" As soon as she said the spiteful words, she regretted them. Why did this man provoke such contradictory reactions in her? It wasn't that old standby of fiction, a love-hate relationship. You don't love a man you've just met; and you certainly don't hate him, either. It was more like attraction and annoyance. How *could* such an appealing man waste his talent on something so dreamy and vague as poetry?

He grinned and twirled the rain-straightened strand of hair back into what he called a kiss curl. "No, *macushla*, I'm practicing for the day I make love to you."

Chapter Two

TO PROVIDE RENTAL housing for its executives and research staff, most of whom were American, Biochem
had bought a cluster of new houses in a small subdivision
near its plant. Miranda shared a three-bedroom buff-
colored stucco house with a biochemist named Linda
Stokes, who was now in Philadelphia on a leave of absence to tend a gravely ill mother.

Miranda and Linda had furnished the house with only
a utilitarian view in mind. Tables and chairs and beds
were a necessity, but Killarney wasn't home and Miranda
wasn't even sure how long she'd be with Biochem. Although her job was a good one, she had applied for a
postdoctoral fellowship at a research institute in New
York. If she got it, she would probably leave the company, with approval for this career move from her men-
tor, Walter Royce.

Wanting to save money but having no time to shop
for good furniture in secondhand stores, the two women
had bought the cheapest furniture available in Cork, the

nearest city. And when the last piece had been delivered, they stood together in the living room and surveyed what they had done.

"It's incredible," Linda had said in an awed tone.

"Godawful," Miranda agreed. "The ugliest I've ever seen. Did we actually *choose* those flimsy end tables with the fancy brass handles?"

Linda nodded solemnly. "You liked that shiny mahogany veneer."

"I couldn't have! Well, maybe I did," Miranda admitted grudgingly. She walked over to the sofa, upholstered in a lurid tropical print, and poked a finger at a large red flower. "Looks poisonous."

Linda had shaken her head. "I think it's those acidy-looking green vines that are poisonous."

"The lamps aren't too bad," Miranda said doubtfully.

"They give light," Linda conceded.

They had gone from room to room, giggling at their purchases. But, they told each other, they hadn't spent a lot of money, and what with work, sightseeing, and other activities, they wouldn't be home that much.

Miranda stood now at the window overlooking a pasture populated in the daytime by glossy brown and white Jerseys. The cows had long since trailed their way to the barn and the failing light was slowly draining the grass of its color. Through a fringe of alders, Miranda could just glimpse the pearly luster of Lough Leane, the largest of the three great lakes of Killarney.

She glanced back into the living room at the clock on the mantel. She should be leaving now for the fifteen-minute drive to Biochem and Brian's poetry reading. But she didn't want to go. She didn't want to hear Brian read his poetry. Poetry was so *personal!* How *could* a man as attractive as Brian O'Bannon stand up in front of a group of people and recite that gushy emotional stuff? But her absence would be noticed, if not in the auditorium, then certainly at the reception for Brian that the Royces had planned in their home afterward.

Miranda turned from the window and reached across one of the passion flowers of the couch for her raincoat. As she belted it around her, all her resistance to attending the poetry reading left her and she suddenly felt buoyant and gay. Raising a wry eyebrow, she thought, you're going to see him again, and that's why you're happy, in spite of the poetry.

Miranda entered Biochem's auditorium ten minutes late on a wave of laughter. She glanced toward the podium. Brian was there—evidently Walter Royce had already finished his introduction and sat down—and whatever the poet had said before she arrived had her colleagues practically rolling in the aisles.

Miranda sidled onto a chair in the last row. Looking around her, she noted that the house was good. Everyone who worked at Biochem—in the plant as well as the research division—was invited to the lectures and performances the cultural-program committee arranged. But the Irish employees, some of whom lived a considerable distance away, usually went home after the day's work, so that it was mostly the Americans and a smattering of others who showed up for the programs. Tonight, however, thanks to O'Bannon's fame, the auditorium was almost full.

More laughter, even louder this time, at something the poet said made Miranda focus, with a fast-beating heart, on Brian himself. His broad shoulders were encased in brown tweed that looked as though it had been worn so many years as to have taken on the shape of the man himself. Something was wrong with his tie again. It wasn't the color; that was a respectable maroon, not fire-engine red. But it was too narrow, too weightless, perhaps, because every time O'Bannon moved his head, the tie swung madly to the left, ending up on his shoulder.

Still, he cut a handsome figure, Miranda thought as she ran her eyes over his hair, glossy under the fluorescent lights; his skin, ruddy with good health; and his glistening starched white shirt; until—and Miranda smiled in near-disbelief—her gaze reached his shoes. One was unmistakably black and the other just as unmistakably brown. Were the shoes what he had just joked about and had she missed the explanation, or was he unaware of his mistake?

Absorbed in these thoughts, Miranda missed Brian's reading of his first poem. But she couldn't ignore the hypnotic spell of his voice for long, and eventually let it draw her into the world he was creating with rhythm and strangely true images and words wrenched from their usual meanings. The poems Brian O'Bannon read that night were spare and taut. The subject matter seemed simple enough as he recited them—an incident on a farm, an old grave, family pictures. When he read a short poem about trout fishing, Miranda thought with a smile that Walter Royce must have appreciated that one; but when Brian's resonant voice came to a firm, quiet stop after each poem, there was a silence in the auditorium that was denser than the absence of sound. Miranda guessed that each poem had an impact on the sensibility of the people there, as it did on hers.

It seemed to her that the poems reflected a man who took other people, but not himself, seriously, and who used common, everyday incidents to arrive at some basic understanding about life. Miranda had the curious impression that each poem was like a cell, complete in itself but part of a whole. Then she thrust the idea aside. What could poetry possibly have in common with biology?

Miranda gleaned an inkling of the events in Brian's life from brief autobiographical explanations he made before reading some poems. He was a farm boy from an old Kerry family. As she had guessed, he had gone to Trinity College, but on a scholarship. His "on the road" poetry had been written during the year he hitchhiked through and worked at odd jobs in the United States. He had loaded cargo in New Orleans, ridden in Texas rodeos, felled trees in Oregon, and crewed from Acapulco to Tasmania on a private yacht.

Miranda raised her dark eyebrows. Now she knew the reason for those big shoulders and the gracefulness of his movements. Whatever else Brian O'Bannon might be, he was a highly physical man. For a moment, a quick lowering of her thick lashes blotted out everything but the unsought image of herself in his arms, her lips delicately parting under his. Then she forced her attention back to his poetry.

The hearty applause O'Bannon received at the end of the program surprised Miranda. Although many of her colleagues enjoyed music and theater, few had ever expressed an interest in poetry. The rigors of a scientific training precluded any extensive study of literature. Miranda herself had often wished, because of her busy schedule, that there were such a thing as a twenty-six-hour day. Not that she'd fritter away the extra hours on poetry, though.

Feeling a little churlish, Miranda sat back while waves of applause broke around her. She didn't consider herself qualified to judge poetry. Moreover, poetry readings, with their connotation of out-of-the-way bookstores with esoteric names and arty "little magazines" seemed inappropriate, as well as time-wasting, for a scientific establishment like Biochem to sponsor.

Miranda succeeded in avoiding Brian and the congratulatory crowd around him, but the quick exit she had planned was slowed by friends wanting to chat a bit on the way out. When she finally stepped out into the night, Brian was there, obviously waiting for her, and her heart gave that absurd little bump it had on their previous encounters.

His hand on her elbow, Brian separated her from the crowd so quickly that she was amazed to find herself suddenly alone with him in the dark, outside the perimeters of Biochem's plant. But that's the way it was in Killarney; except for the touristy little town of Killarney itself, you were always in the country.

"I would have thought you'd still be shaking hands," Miranda said tartly. "Your poetry reading was obviously a great success."

"Did *you* like it?" he asked.

"I don't read poetry; therefore, I can't judge it."

"I'm not asking you to judge it, woman. Did you like it, I asked?"

She hesitated, some tremendous inner wall of resistance preventing her from saying yes, she had liked his poetry.

"Then you didn't," he said bitterly.

"Does it matter?"

"Of course it matters. I was reading the poems to you."

Don't, Miranda thought. Don't involve me in your life like that. I have my own world. I don't want yours.

"Ah, well," he said lightly, "poetry does take a bit of getting used to. While we're waiting, would you mind giving me a lift to the Royces' house? I find myself without transportation at the moment."

"I'd be glad to take you." Miranda coughed discreetly. "Did you know that you've got one black shoe and one brown shoe on?"

"Sure and I have no sartorial sense at all. I think I'm in need of a wife."

"Are you going to the reception like that?"

"My cottage isn't far from Yanktown, as the locals call the place where you Americans live." A seductive note crept into his voice. "If my appearance disturbs you, we can go there and I'll change."

A ridiculous little shiver ran through Miranda at the news that he lived close to her, but all she said was, *"I wouldn't care if you went to the party barefoot."*

They reached her car, and he opened the door on the passenger side for her.

"I'm driving," she remonstrated.

"Sure and the road's full of potholes this time of night. Toss me the keys and I'll save you the trouble."

Laughing, she took her car keys out of her raincoat pocket and handed them over. As she sat beside him, the green lights of the dash creating a cozy little world in the darkness for just the two of them, Miranda's senses were inflamed by his nearness, by the silhouette of his handsome profile, and by his strong, sun-browned hand so close to her knee when he moved the shift stick. If he stopped the car and put his arms around her now, she knew she wouldn't resist.

But they were soon part of the stream of cars pulling up in front of the Royces'. It was the largest of the American-owned houses, a stopping-off place for Walter and Janet's many offspring when they went backpacking in Switzerland or rode the trains on a student Eurailpass or left a grandchild or two to be doted over. During the long stretches of time when she and Walter were alone, Janet occupied herself with "antiquing." What Walter referred to as "Mother's junk"—silver salt cellars lined with blue glass, porcelain scent bottles, cut glass decanters with mushroom-shaped stoppers—filled a lighted étagère in the foyer. Some of the pieces, Miranda thought, showed that Janet had a very shrewd eye.

That same shrewd eye now examined Miranda and Brian as they entered the house. What does she see? Miranda wondered. Do I look flushed; excited? How will she interpret that blissfully contented look of Brian's?

Miranda watched him as he exchanged the usual social banalities with his hostess and the guests who crowded around to compliment him on the poetry reading, until finally she turned away, embarrassed. Everywhere he went and regardless of whom he was speaking to, his gaze kept returning to her. She saw people smile, and one or two obviously commented on his attentions.

Flustered and a little annoyed and yet pleased all at the same time, Miranda followed Janet's short, plumpish figure, which was swathed in a plaid taffeta evening skirt, into the kitchen.

"Can I help?" Miranda asked, smiling at the two "temps"—one loading a tray with canapés, the other washing glasses in the sink.

"No, dear. I just came in to see how the smoked salmon was holding out. That's a pretty dress," Janet said absently, glancing at the simple but well-cut sheer red wool Miranda was wearing.

"Thank you. I bought it in Cork just a few days ago."

Janet smiled knowingly. "A new dress for Brian's poetry reading?"

Nettled by her friend's assumption, Miranda shook her head and replied, "For *your* cocktail party."

Paying not the slightest attention to Miranda's answer, Janet continued on her own track. "I can see by the way he looks at you that Brian is interested in you. I hope you're not interested in him—seriously, I mean."

Miranda laughed. "I've only just met the man, Janet."

"That doesn't mean anything," the older woman replied placidly, poking sprigs of parsley into place on a serving dish. "Walter proposed on our first date, and we've been married over thirty-five years."

"Well, there's no danger of that in this case."

"Good." The small, Cupid's-bow lips closed decisively over the word. "I'm glad to hear it."

"Why?" Miranda asked curiously.

Janet laughed. "My dear, given your dedication to science, you could never be happy with anyone but a scientist."

"I'm divorced from a scientist," Miranda reminded her ruefully.

"Well, of course! You and Craig never even saw each other. What do you think would have happened to Walter's and my marriage if we'd lived in different cities?"

"I suppose you wouldn't have had seven children," Miranda said with wide-eyed innocence.

"Eight," Janet answered and, kissing Miranda on the cheek, rustled out to mingle with her guests.

Unexpectedly irritated by Janet's interference yet unwilling to return to the living room and Brian, Miranda stepped out the rear kitchen door and walked into the back garden. The night was cool but not cold. A sweater would have been welcome, but lacking one, Miranda folded her arms around herself. She drew a deep breath of the moist air, pungent with the earthy smell of the land. Then Brian's voice was close beside her, and she admitted to herself that she had known he would come.

"It's a dull party without you," he said. "What are you doing out here?"

"So you find scientists dull," she said, turning and facing him.

"When they talk shop, yes; but I heard some interesting gossip, too."

"Oh?" she asked on a rising inflection.

"Someone mentioned that your ex-husband is a good scientist."

"Yes, Craig is a talented researcher," Miranda said in a flat tone.

"Obviously, he was less talented as a husband."

Miranda shrugged. "Our marriage failed, but I can't say it was all Craig's fault."

"Is that how you regard marriage—as a success or

failure?" His voice rang with surprise.

"Well, I don't give out grades one to ten," Miranda said defensively, "but . . ."

"You do give a pass or a fail," Brian interrupted. "And I have half an idea you're a hard marker. What was wrong with your marriage, *macushla?*"

"I don't know," she said tentatively, groping for objectivity and accuracy even as she talked. "I honestly don't know. We lived apart much of the time because we had jobs in different cities and I always give that as the reason, but I'm not sure that it was."

"Did you love him?"

"I think so. I cared about him, as I'm sure he did about me. We had interests in common . . . but really, is this any of your business?"

She tightened her arms across her breasts and stepped back, away from him. Why did she always end up doing what this man wanted, even to babbling about her failed marriage?

"Everything about you is my business," he said feelingly.

She started to say, "No, it isn't!" but his mouth stopped her, sealing her half-opened lips in a kiss that drained her of all desire to analyze or object or explain. She shivered, but he misunderstood.

"You're cold," he said. He put his hands on hers and gently removed her arms from across her breasts. Then he put his hands on her waist and pulled her close to him. He wrapped his tweed jacket around them both.

She could feel the beat of his heart and his overwhelmingly male body hard against hers. She wound her arms around his waist and stood for a moment, giving herself over to the feel of his lean muscled torso and the starchy smell of his shirt and the different, but no less appealing smell of his tweed jacket, impregnated with the faint smoky odor of a wood fire. She thrilled to him, wanted him, longed for more of him; and the knowledge that he wanted her, too, sent deep shivers up and down her spine.

His lips touched her hair, then trailed down to her ear. He squeezed a delicious kiss into its small orifice, then whispered, "I have to go back to the party. I'm the guest of honor," he added with a chuckle. "Come with me. You'll catch your death out here, if you don't."

"I will—in a few minutes."

He put his finger under her chin and raised her face to his again. "You don't have a man in there you're hiding me from, do you?"

"Oh, sure," Miranda answered with a laugh. "I have men all over the place."

"With your looks, I wouldn't be surprised," Brian muttered. "I think I'll go in and announce that you're coming as soon as you've fixed yourself up a bit."

"Don't! It would upset Janet no end," Miranda said lightly. "She thinks a scientist, like her Walter, is the only man for me."

"The poor woman's probably never been kissed by a poet." His lips found hers again, pressing them fervently yet gently. Then, when they had parted under his tender assault, he caressed their soft underside with his velvety tongue. Each flickering, probing touch was exquisitely tantalizing. And when his tongue smoothly glided deep into the hollows of her eager mouth, she thrilled to the delightful sensation.

She could feel all the regret in his body when he pulled away from her. His hands firm on her slim sides, he brushed her lips once more with his. "Come soon," he whispered, "or I'll have nothing beautiful to rest my eyes on."

"I'd like to speak to you about that," Miranda said. "It's embarrassing and causes comment when you keep looking at me."

"Sure and how can I help it, lovely as you are?"

"Must you always have the last word?" she asked, exasperated, but his rapid stride had taken him out of earshot. Wrapping her arms about herself again, Miranda started to pace back and forth to keep warm. She really had to stop right where she was with Brian, she thought. The relationship was warming up much too fast. Attractive though he was, she had no intention of going to bed with him. Nor was she going to fall in love with him. She liked him, but their worlds were so different that any lasting relationship would be impossible.

And yet, she thought wistfully, she wanted to love and be loved by a man again. It wasn't that she felt incomplete without a man, and she certainly didn't need a husband to give her status. But marriage had accorded her a glimpse of the joyful intimacy possible between a man and a woman. Although her own brief union hadn't fulfilled that promise, Miranda knew with a steady upsurging beat of optimism that she would find the right partner some time. She would have to be careful, however, because another mistake could turn her life into a disaster. This made Brian O'Bannon, to whose party she should be returning at that very moment, a definite danger, because what else could the man be for her but a mistake?

Sighing, Miranda went back into the house and made her way to the living room. Folding cold hands around the goblet of champagne one of the black-frocked maids offered her, Miranda stood a moment savoring the warmth of the brightly lit room and the gaiety of the successful party. Many of the guests were now helping themselves to a buffet of Galway oysters, local salmon, roast beef, and salads, and little groups of plate balancers sat here and there, flashing their forks in the air as they talked and ate.

A separate table had been set up for Irish coffee, and

Mary, the Royces' regular maid, was expertly preparing the drink in gold-edged stemmed glassware with a green shamrock on the bowl. She put a heaping teaspoon of brown sugar into a previously warmed glass and added enough hot black coffee, approximately a cup, to dissolve the sugar. She stirred it, then added Irish whisky to within an inch of the brim. Holding a teaspoon, curved side up, across the glass, she next poured a tablespoon of thick chilled cream slowly over the spoon and let it float on top, unstirred, so that the hot, whisky-laced coffee would be drunk through the chilled cream.

Miranda saw Brian standing with Royce and several other men from the research department, talking vigorously, seemingly expounding on a subject that held the others in rapt attention. She was curious. What could Brian be saying that would interest these biologists so much?

As Miranda walked toward the men, her eyes met Brian's. The tender yet ardent look in their dark blue depths made her turn her head aside, but she could feel her high, full young breasts push against the sheer wool of her dress, as though her whole body strained to press itself against his.

Walter Royce welcomed her into the circle. "You've come at a good time, Miranda. We've been having a most interesting discussion about poetry and science. Brian's been showing us that they're not so different as one might suppose." Walter's eyes suddenly sparkled behind his rimless glasses. "I've just had a brilliant idea— brilliant even for me," he added with a laugh. "How would you like to enlarge on what you've just been telling us, Brian, and present your ideas to a larger group?"

"What did you have in mind, sir?" Brian asked.

"Well, this is only tentative, of course," Walter began, furrowing his brow, "and it's subject to the decision of the committee for Biochem's cultural program, but how about a series of lectures explaining poetry to scientists? Judging from the response to your reading tonight and the interest I've heard expressed here at the party, I'm sure such a series of talks would be popular. What do you think?" he asked, looking around at the small group.

Miranda's heart suddenly started to beat painfully fast. Her body seemed to be reacting to Walter's suggestion before she could even marshal her thoughts. She thought it was a silly idea, but did one's heart go like a triphammer just because one disagreed with a proposal? Hers never had, and she had sat in on countless conferences. She listened with dismay as the others expressed their approval and Brian said he'd be glad to undertake such a series of lectures.

"Miranda," Walter said, "you've been awfully quiet. What do you think of the idea?"

"Well, I really can't see what scientists—or anyone else, for that matter, except poets and English majors—can hope to gain from studying poetry. I mean, what use does it have in the modern world?" Miranda was shocked by the vehemence of her tone. She was angry with herself and felt somehow betrayed by the intensity of the nameless emotion Walter's proposal had provoked in her. She was driven now to justifying herself and continued with flushed face and furiously beating heart to point out that *she* didn't have the time to waste on poetry lectures and she was sure not many others did, either; that she didn't want to offend Mr. O'Bannon, but everyone had his own sphere of work and what was the point of trying to bring them together?

Her tirade was met with surprised looks that Miranda could well understand. She rarely allowed her emotions to enter the arena of ideas; and never like this. She felt a little sick at having exposed herself, but quickly countered this feeling with the rationalization that she was among friends. However, this knowledge didn't lessen

the sensation she had of being poised over a chasm—
the chaos of the unknown self. *Why* had she reacted so
strongly to Walter's idea of Brian's giving lectures about
poetry?

"I'm sorry you feel that way, Miranda," Walter said.
"But I think you're going to be outvoted, and you don't
have to come to the lectures," he added with a smile.

Miranda nodded dumbly, covered with shame and
confusion. She had been avoiding Brian's eyes, but now
she looked up at him. A furrow between his dark brows
suddenly smoothed itself out and a mischievous gleam
sparkled in his eyes, like sunlight on blue water.

"I can take care of the poetry end all right," he said,
"but my science is pretty weak. Would you care to collaborate on these lectures with me, Miranda? You could
be the goddess of science and I would be the humble
servant of poetry."

Miranda stared at him in amazement. Damn him and
his Kerry lilt and the laugh in his eyes! He had outfoxed
her. Then she narrowed her eyes for a moment. He had
also thrown down the gauntlet to her. Her spine stiffened
and she raised a fighting chin, so that when Walter Royce
said, "That's a good idea. What do you say, Miranda?
It'll give you a chance to learn about poetry from the
inside; maybe change your opinion," she was able to
answer him with cool self-control.

"I'll be glad to give Mr. O'Bannon whatever assis-
tance I can, although I doubt that I would ever be interested in poetry—or its not nearly humble enough
servants."

Chapter Three

"THE BIOCHEM CONFERENCE ROOM!"

"My place, *macushla.*"

"I won't go to your cottage."

"I've got all my notes and books here."

Miranda slammed the phone down. Thrusting her fists
hard into her apron pockets, she jumped up and began
to pace the living room floor. He was incredible—un-
trustworthy, ungentlemanly, and unbearable. He had
blarneyed everyone into thinking these poetry and science
lectures were the greatest thing since penicillin. He had
maneuvered her into helping him. Now he was insisting
that they work on the lectures not in the neutral sur-
roundings of Biochem's conference room but in his cottage—complete, of course, with a fireplace and a couch
and . . . and . . . Irish coffee, no doubt, as a perfect aid to
seduction, getting her drunk and keeping her awake all
at the same time.

Miranda picked a fringed shiny pink pillow off the
couch and hurled it to the floor. Well, she wouldn't go.

She launched a kick at a mud-brown synthetic leather hassock. It was beyond the call of duty. No one could expect it of her.

Then she plopped herself down on the hassock and stretched her long legs out in front of her. She folded her hands behind her head, leaned her back against the overstuffed chair, and smiled. Brian's insistence on their working at his place could hardly be called nefarious. Miranda's smile deepened. She pointed her toes and looked down at them. It was exciting, knowing that a man as handsome and famous as Brian O'Bannon had designs on her. Besides, what an unsophisticated fool she'd look if she shied away from working in the poet's home. Resolutely, Miranda put her feet on the floor and stood up. She went to the phone and dialed Brian's number. But no Irish coffee! she warned herself.

"I'll come get you," he said.

"That's not necessary. Just give me a time, and I'll be there."

"You'll never find the place. It's just a cottage in the hills behind Yanktown. You don't know the road, and if the gentry are in a foul mood they might lead your car astray."

"The gentry?"

"That's what we call the 'wee people,' the *slooa shee*, or fairies. They're quick to take offense and must be mentioned in a respectful manner, or watch out . . ."

"I'll do that," Miranda said dryly.

"Suppose I pick you up at seven, then?"

Miranda could hear the glee in his voice. He was practically rubbing his hands together, she fumed. Drat the man! Didn't he ever lose?

Miranda liked to cook, but when she wasn't entertaining confined herself to simple dishes like the Irish stew she now removed from the oven. The casserole of lamb, potatoes, carrots, and onions was nourishing and would last several days. Besides, she thought, sniffing appreciatively, it was delicious.

Meals were the worst time for loneliness. Miranda had discovered that when she and Craig took jobs in different cities. It seemed to her then that she missed him more at dinner than in bed. Thinking of that time now as she placed a bowl of stew on the table, she grimaced. From the very beginning, Craig's lovemaking had been somewhat perfunctory. He regarded the minutes spent in bed as time stolen from his work—from the reading he had to do, the paper he was writing for a professional journal, the analysis of computer data. And when their time together shrank to weekends that began with fatigue, waiting for delayed planes, and the anxiety of making connections, any chance for improvement disappeared. A serious sense of urgency, even duty, entered their lovemaking. It became not too unlike going to the dentist, Miranda thought, breaking off a piece of the brown soda bread she had baked the week before and spreading country-fresh yellow butter on it.

Sighing, she placed a scientific journal beside her plate. She had learned long ago that reading helped when one had to eat alone. Come to think of it, she read in bed, too. You've become a great reader, Miranda, my girl. Maybe it's time you threw away the books and got yourself a man. But not just any man! Of course not, dummy; someone you can discuss ideas with. Someone like Craig? Don't be idiotic. Not all scientists are like Craig. But it has to be a scientist; Janet was right, then. Of course it has to be a scientist. There's more to marriage than bed. There's conversation, friends, a community of ideas. Then why are you going to a certain poet's cottage in the middle of the night?

Miranda slammed the journal shut. It's not the middle of the night, she rebuked herself. It's only half past six. I'll be home before ten. Reminded of the time, she got up quickly and put what was left of the stew in the refrigerator. Then she went into her bedroom and opened the closet door. What did one wear to a nonseduction?

She decided on plaid, which she associated with school uniforms. She reached way behind her other clothes and pulled out a purple plaid wool skirt that buttoned down the front. It was a mistake, bought when she first arrived in Ireland for warmth and because it was a bargain. Over that, she put a lavender wool turtleneck.

She drew her thick blond hair severely back and tied it with a narrow black ribbon. Looking at herself in the mirror, she wavered. Without makeup and with her hair like that, she had the wan look of an overgrown schoolgirl. If she had a white lab coat on, she'd be the quintessential stereotype of the sexless woman scientist. Miranda wrinkled her nose in distaste. That woman wasn't her, and it hurt to go out looking like this. But it was all for a good cause, she reminded herself.

She was just hanging up the linen tea towel when she heard a roar that sounded like ground-level thunder. It reached a climax as it got closer, then died down and abruptly stopped. Miranda ran to the front window just in time to see a helmeted, leather-clad figure throw a long, muscled leg over the saddle of his motorcycle and stand upright in front of her house. He took off the helmet and ran his fingers through his dark hair.

Somehow, a motorcycle didn't seem the right vehicle for a poet, and Miranda was still a little wide-eyed as she watched Brian come up the walk. The tight leather jacket that ended at his waist made his shoulders look even broader, his legs longer. He moved with the natural grace of a man used to doing things with his body. He also, Miranda now noticed, was carrying two helmets—one tucked under each arm. Miranda swallowed hard. She had never ridden a motorcycle for the very good reason that she was afraid. And she was not going to now. Mr. Brian O'Bannon, Ireland's leading poet and Hell's Angel, could go back up the hill to his cottage alone. She would use her car, like any other sensible person.

Offense, everyone knew, was the best defense. So when she opened the door to him, Miranda said, "How can you possibly justify polluting the beautiful countryside with that thing?"

"Ah, it's not that bad," he said cajolingly. "After all, there's only one of me."

"Thank heavens for that!" Miranda opened the door wider. "Won't you come in?"

"I don't know," he answered, looking her up and down with a puzzled expression. "Are you ready?"

"Yes. If you'll wait a minute, I'll get my car out of the garage and follow you up the hill."

"There's no need. You can sit on the rear saddle," he said with a nod toward the motorbike.

"I don't like motorcycles," she said flatly.

"You don't know what you're missing. When you're in a car, you're always in a compartment, separated from what's around you. Everything you see through that windshield is just telly scenery. But on a motorbike, the frame is gone. You're *part* of the scenery."

"Sure, wrapped around a tree; pushing up daisies."

"Not with me, you won't be."

"I'm sorry, Brian. I'm engaged in an important research project. I can't afford to be laid up in Killarney General."

"You're afraid."

"Right. I'm the coward of the month—every month—when it comes to motorcycles. Now may I get my car out of the garage?"

He barred her way at the door, and before she could stop him he had placed one of the helmets on her head.

"What are you doing?" Her voice rose with surprise and anger.

Silently, he stepped back and looked at her. He shook his head. "I don't like it," he said.

"Well, neither do I." She raised her hands to remove the helmet and his long fingers closed over hers, warming her with the glow she felt whenever he touched her. Somehow the helmet ended up in his hand and she thought, Natch! He hasn't lost a round yet. His other hand reached around her, and her hair fell loose across her neck. In a purely instinctive gesture, she tossed her head back, reveling for a moment in the freedom.

She caught the glint of admiration in his eyes; then he plopped the helmet back on her head.

"That's better," he said brusquely. "You looked a bit like a skinned rabbit the other way. We can go now."

"I told you, Brian, I'm not going on the motorcycle!"

He took her hands then and placed them on his waist. "You'll be riding like that, putting all your trust in me, and I haven't had an accident yet. It's still light, now and the cottage isn't far. And wouldn't it be a marvelous new experience for you?"

His sea-dark eyes held hers, assuring her that what he had just said was true. But when she followed him down the walk and stood alongside the motorbike, she was afraid again. The shiny machine was so big and powerful; so terribly, ruthlessly masculine looking. She hung back, but Brian held his hand out to her as though it was the most natural thing in the world for her to mount the motorcycle. When they were both astride, he reached behind for her hands and drew her arms around his waist.

"Hang on!" he shouted. He pumped twice on the kick starter. With a deafening *vroom-vroom,* the machine leaped from the curb and hurtled down the road with what seemed to Miranda like supersonic speed. Rigid with fear, she clutched Brian and stared catatonically ahead. What if they ran into one of those flocks of mad, asphalt-loving sheep that populated Irish roads? They might even meet that lone Irish motorist defending his right, according to national custom, to the center of the road.

Gradually, however, Miranda relaxed and began to enjoy the ride. She relished the evening breeze on her face, the lingering streak of pink in the west, the nearness of everything—from the road just below her feet to the cows jingling along the side of it to the barn. Brian had been right. She did feel more a part of her physical world on the motorcycle than in a car.

It was her trust in Brian, Miranda admitted, that made her pleasure possible. Even when the road became hilly and twisting, the skill with which he banked into the turns removed any lingering doubt she had about her safety. Sitting so close to him, her whole upper torso pressed to his, Miranda began to feel part of a single being—she and Brian and the machine were as one. With powerful thrusts, the motorcycle was carrying them further and further into a private world of their own—a world of trees and streams and a darkening sky.

He turned and yelled something at her, but his words were carried away by the wind, and she smiled and shook her head at him. Then he was slowing down. He steered the motorbike into a clearing in a grove of beeches and lifted her off the rear seat.

His hands slipped up her sides and nudged the crescent curves of her breasts. A look of infinite longing darkened his eyes.

"You're like a promise," he whispered. "Like the moon when it's new."

His lips descended to hers, but she pulled away, her eyes dancing. "Not all promises are fulfilled."

"I can wait, *macushla*," he said softly. He put his finger on his lips then and, taking her hand, led her through the woods until they came to a small lake, black and deep looking. The air held the hush of early evening. Silently, as Brian and Miranda watched, four white swans moved majestically across the dark glassy surface.

"They don't look real," Miranda said, awed by the mysterious beauty of the place.

"They are, but I have no idea where they came from or why they stay, except that they must get enough food and are safe here." He glanced away from the lake and looked down into her face. "Do you know the story of the children of Lir?"

"No," Miranda said in a low voice. In spite of her achievement in science, she always felt a little embarrassed by her lack of knowledge about literature. There simply had never been time. It was all she could do to keep up with the flood of information in her own field.

"I would have been surprised if you did, as it's an old Irish legend," Brian said with a grin. "King Lir had four children, three boys and a girl, of whom their stepmother Aoife was very jealous. Aoife decided to kill the children and brought them to a lake for that purpose. But her courage failed her and instead she told the children to bathe in the lake. When they entered the water, she raised a druidic wand and changed them into four white swans, condemned to wander for nine hundred years over the waters of Ireland. As soon as she had performed this evil deed, Aoife was filled with remorse. She allowed the children to retain their human speech and also gave them the gift of beautiful song.

"King Lir set out to find his missing children, and as he approached the lake he heard the swans speaking with human voices. He asked them who they were, and when he learned they were his children he was overcome with grief. He stayed by the lake till the swans flew away. Then he made it a law that no swan should be killed in Ireland from that day on."

"And the queen? Did Lir do anything to her?" Miranda questioned, oddly enchanted by the tale.

"Aoife was punished by her own father, who turned her into an air-demon, and the children were released from the magic spell. But when the feathers fell from their bodies, it was seen that they were withered and feeble, and they died shortly afterward."

"That's a sad story," Miranda said with sincerity.

Brian nodded. "But with a happy ending. Ever since then, it's been against the law in Ireland to kill a swan."

"Really?" she asked skeptically.

"It's forbidden to kill swans—that part is true, anyway. We should be getting along," he continued. But he just stood there, looking at her curiously. "You like it here, don't you?"

"Yes. There's a kind of magic about it. I half expect to hear the swans sing," she said with a laugh. Then, more seriously, she asked, "Is there a connection between the Irish King Lir and Shakespeare's King Lear?"

"It's believed that there is." A teasing smile lit his face. "You'll be switching over from science to literary scholarship soon, I suppose."

Miranda shook her head emphatically. "I like theories that can be proved, one way or the other, and results that are useful to people."

With a quizzical look, he put his hand on her arm and they walked back through the woods. They mounted the motorcycle again and didn't stop until they reached a cabin of rough fieldstone standing alone in a copse of mountain ash.

"I built it myself," Brian said proudly. "Wait till you see the inside."

The entire cabin consisted of one large room, with, as Miranda had anticipated, a fireplace—a large, open one with a brick hearth. The walls were hung with colorful woven designs, and rugs covered a flagstone floor.

"It's lovely," Miranda said. "Spacious and yet warm. How did you know how to build it?"

"I'd done construction work here and there, and the rest I learned as I had to. Here, I'll make a fire."

As he knelt down and busied himself with paper and wood, Miranda looked around. One corner, furnished with a typewriter, a desk, and a file cabinet, was obviously work space. A narrow bed covered with a brown corduroy throw occupied a windowed alcove. A steady low hum disclosed the whereabouts of the kitchen refrigerator behind a folding wooden screen. The center of the room was furnished with modern, comfortable-looking chairs and sofas and conveniently placed tables and lamps. But the predominant feature of the room was the books. They filled bookcases and wall shelves, stood in square phalanxes on the floor, and leaned towerlike against the walls.

A mirror on the wall reflected Miranda's image. The motorcycle ride had fired her cheeks to a high, rosy glow. Her dark eyes shone, and her hair cascaded in a straight blond waterfall to her shoulders. The lavender sweater molded her breasts more than she had realized when she chose it, and looking down, she discovered that she had forgotten about the last three skirt buttons, undone for her comfort on the motorcycle.

She turned just as Brian stood up, the first bright flames of a wood fire behind him. The look in his eyes showed he had reached the same conclusion about her clothes that she had.

Some nonseductive outfit! she thought.

"Why don't you sit down here in front of the fire while I make us some Irish coffee." He indicated the large overstuffed couch facing the fireplace.

But Miranda didn't sit down. A look of total disbelief showed on her face. All her predictions—the fire, the couch, and the Irish coffee—were coming true.

"I thought we were going to work on your first poetry and science lecture."

"We are, but you're not going to be very effective in your current tense state."

"Tense!" Miranda cried. "What makes you think I'm tense?"

"Just listen to your voice. You're practically screaming."

"So would you be if someone said you were tense when you weren't."

"Now you're making your hands into fists."

"I'll let *you* guess why. May we get started, please? Tomorrow's a work day." She eyed the books. "For some people, anyway."

"But not for worthless layabout poets who do nothing but read books all day." His blue eyes narrowed in amusement and laugh wrinkles fanned out on his fair skin. "All right, since you insist. But I still advise the couch instead of that desk you keep looking at. What we're going to be doing is sitting around, exchanging ideas." He got a pad of yellow lined paper, and since they were *his* poetry and science lectures anyway, Miranda sat down, choosing a far corner of the large sofa and decorously buttoning her skirt.

An hour later, several pages were filled with Brian's bold scrawl, answers to the questions about science he had put to Miranda. Time had passed quickly in the rapid flash of ideas and almost instant communication that occurred between them.

"Time to stretch," Brian said, reaching over and pulling Miranda up by her hands. His arm lightly around her waist, he led her to a window. "I want you to listen to something," he said. He pushed the upper half of the double-hung window open, and suddenly the night was filled with the sound of running, rushing water.

Miranda smiled with pleasure. "You've got a river at your back door!"

"Practically. Sometimes you can see deer there. The red deer of Killarney are the only surviving herds from the original deer population hunted by the Celts. They come down from the hills to drink at the river. And there are salmon—the biggest salmon in Ireland, and that's no blarney."

Miranda recalled the giant reddish-gold salmon on the wall of Walter Royce's office, then remembered the alacrity with which Walter had jumped at Brian's suggestion that she help with the lectures. For one idle, jesting moment she wondered if Walter and Brian had secretly made all the arrangements beforehand. Had Walter traded her for a salmon?

The idea seemed so comical that Miranda could barely suppress a smile.

"Are you laughing at my river?" Brian asked.

Now laughing openly, Miranda shook her head.

"You are! Do you know what the river god did to mortals who offended him? I mean women."

Even though she knew he was just fooling, Miranda felt a thrill of mingled fear and anticipation run up and down her spine. What was he going to do to her? She wet her lips nervously with the tip of her tongue as she stood and watched him.

He returned her look, his eyes holding hers while he said in a voice slowed by emotion, "If the woman was beautiful, the god demanded that she marry him."

"And if she refused?"

His eyes were laughing at her now like sunlit blue water. "The river god got her anyway. She was thrown in without benefit of ceremony."

"Doesn't sound as though the poor girl had much of a chance."

"She didn't. We river gods are ruthless once we've made up our minds."

Miranda's heart began to beat fast. She turned her head away for a moment, then faced Brian again. "Is that a genuine legend?" she asked suspiciously.

"Actually, no." He grinned with smug satisfaction.

"It's a bit of blarney I made up for the exigencies of the moment."

She moved away from him, back toward the center of the room. "I'd like to go home now, if you don't mind. You have at least a week before the first lecture. I can help you another time."

Brian caught up with her. Placing his hands on her shoulders, he turned her around. "You're upset with me."

"Not at all." She glanced at her watch. "As I said before, it's time I got back."

His eyes surveyed her, and he shook his head. "No, that isn't it. You're not telling me the truth."

"The truth?" she said vehemently. "I thought it was blarney that counted."

"And what's wrong with blarney, *macushla?* It's just your American baloney dressed up with a bit of Irish eloquence and wit."

Miranda refused to be mollified. There seemed to be an anger deep within her that she couldn't reach with reason. Feeling she was on dangerous ground but not caring, she said, "And poetry's just another form of blarney, isn't it?"

The blue seemed to leave his eyes with the sudden coldness that came into them, and his voice was bitter with hurt. *"Blarney* is a 'witty retort' or 'flattery' or even what we call a 'soft deception.' There's no blarney in my feelings for you; there's only truth. And there's no blarney in my poetry. Honesty of feeling is my substance and my goal, precision and clarity my means."

Miranda felt ashamed. She had never impugned anyone's calling before. A person might do his job well or he might do it badly, but whatever he did was, in a sense, him and therefore to be respected.

His tone merely curious now, Brian asked, "What do you have against poetry?" A disarming smile that made Miranda's heart leap up stole across his face. "Most

people don't read it, don't buy it—unfortunately—and
don't pay any attention to poets at all. But you seem
actually to dislike it."

"I don't dislike poetry. It's just that I'm concerned
with facts—hard, observable, provable facts. I don't like
things to be wishy-washy."

"Poetry is the most exact of all the literary arts," he
gently reproved her. "It's also the oldest language we
have, the most elemental and the most natural expression
of ourselves as human beings."

There was a searching look in his eyes that infuriated
Miranda. This detached, objective examination of her
motives was not at all what she wanted from him. What
do you want? she asked herself.

"I think you're afraid," he continued. "But of what,
I can't for the life of me figure out."

"Afraid?" she could only repeat.

"Yes," he said, studying her. "I'm sure of it." He
took a step forward and folded his arms around her. She
felt their strength across her back, and his chest hard
against her soft, mounding breasts. This was it, she
thought, this was what she wanted from him. Then she
repudiated her desire, twisting her head so that he couldn't
reach her lips. She didn't want to go to bed with him,
and she wasn't going to fall in love with him. What *could*
she do with him, this Irish poet who was crooning, "Ssh,
stop thinking, *macushla*. Let yourself go a little. Sure
and you're just a bundle of nerves."

Nervous? Put a little blarney in your life. Maybe she
could sell that to an advertising agency. Miranda smiled
in amused acceptance of defeat.

"That's better, darling," he whispered, his breath warm
in her ear. He took her lips then in a long ardent kiss
that kept changing into something better and more wonderful until finally he lightly brushed his lips over hers.
"I'm putting them back the way they were, *macushla*,

so you don't leave here looking as though you have been made love to by some rude fellow."

Miranda laughed, and he kissed her again. "You're delicious when you laugh, do you know that? Delectable, with your vanilla hair and chocolate eyes. You're just asking to be eaten."

"No, I'm not," Miranda half screamed, half laughed. But he was already nibbling at her, his teeth soft on her ear, then veering off to pull gently at her lower lip so that his tongue could taste it in slow, confident licks. Both of his strong hands were sliding up under her arms now and she gave her breasts willingly to them, reveling in the flow of her female energy into his hands. All her senses exquisitely alive to the thrilling movements of his hands and his strong thighs against hers, Miranda again sought his mouth and its sweet closing over hers.

"You'd best stay here tonight," he said thickly against her hair. "It gets pretty foggy on the hill."

She put her hands against his chest and pushed him away. "I've heard there's no fog in Ireland. That's just more of your blarney."

"You can't blame a man for trying," Brian said with a grin. "Suppose I refused to take you back to Killarney," he added lightly.

"You wouldn't. It wouldn't be gentlemanly."

"You're right about that. Even so, it would be better if you stayed. That road's none too safe in the dark. You can take the bed and I'll doss down on the couch."

It was a temptation. She didn't relish the trip back down those narrow twisting roads on a motorcycle, now that it was night.

As she hesitated, Brian said offhandedly, "Of course if you don't trust me . . . or yourself . . ."

"Oh, I trust myself," she interrupted.

"Good, then you'll stay. I'll get more blankets."

Chapter Four

WHILE HE RUMMAGED around in a cupboard built high on one wall, Miranda stared with wonder into the fire. He had done it again—gotten his own way.

He loaned her a pair of his pajamas and a fresh toothbrush, and she undressed in the small bathroom that opened off the main room. The pajamas were ridiculously big on her. The V neck of the top plunged practically to her midriff. The sleeves and pant legs were clownishly long, and she had to knot the pants at the waist to keep them on her.

Feeling as much undressed as dressed, she finally returned to the living room, now lit only by the fire, and started to make a beeline for the alcove bed.

When Brian saw her, one hand clutching the pajama top across her chest, the other holding up the pants, he burst into laughter. "You'll never make it across the room like that," he said. "Let me help you."

Ignoring the pool of flannel at her feet where the pajama legs had unrolled again, Miranda threw her head back and said proudly, "It really isn't necessary."

The dark room was dancing with firelight. The gentle murmur of the river outside entered through the partly opened window. There was a mystery and excitement in the night that transformed the cabin into a primitive cave.

Miranda had to force a cool smile to her lips as Brian approached her, but her smile faded and she felt her eyes darken with desire when he touched her.

After he had solemnly rolled the sleeves up her arms and bent down for the trouser legs, he stepped back. "There," he said. "I think you stand a better chance now." His voice was harsh and his eyes glanced off her, as though he was afraid of his own need.

She took a step forward, and the pajama legs came down again.

This time his laugh was merry and free. "Sure you're as hobbled as a grazing horse. I'll have to carry you, or we'll never get to bed at all tonight."

The loose pajamas were hardly clothes at all, and when she felt one strong arm under her thighs and the other under her arms as he swooped her up into the air, Miranda knew a stab of excitement that pierced her whole body. She wound her arms tightly around his neck, and the pajama top slid off one shoulder. Brian stopped and looked down at her, and Miranda could see by the light of the fire the fierce longing in his eyes.

His lips flew to hers, pressing their fullness into a sweet harvest of delight. Her eyes fluttered closed, and he laid his lips against each full, finely carved eyelid. Then he wove a garland of kisses around her neck and shoulder. He bent his lips to her breast, made rosy by the firelight, and murmured as he took the taut nipple in his mouth, "You're pink as the western sky, and this is your evening star."

As his mouth moved over the soft swell of her breast, it left a trail of delicious excitement and an aching longing in her. She was taut with passion, with desiring him. He sought her lips again in a thrusting, urgent, powerful kiss that told her exactly what he wanted of her. Then he lifted his mouth slowly, reluctantly, from her trembling lips and said hoarsely, "You're my guest, *macushla*. I'd best finish what I started." With a few steps, he reached the narrow bed. He laid her gently down on it and walked away.

Miranda turned to the wall so she couldn't see the mound his long body made under the blanket on the couch. She consciously blotted out the sound of his breathing so close to hers and ignored the tempestuous longing that tore at her. Making her mind a sieve for all the images and impressions that crowded into it, she gradually induced sleep.

When Miranda woke up, it was still dark outside. She lay still for a moment, listening. She realized the sounds she was hearing must have been the ones that awakened her. There seemed to be a rustling of leaves on the ground, then something that sounded like snuffling followed by a repeated scraping noise she couldn't identify. She looked out the window by her bed but could see nothing except trees.

The sounds were repeated, and Miranda wondered if there wasn't something she should do about them. The pants of the pajamas Brian had loaned her lay in a tangled heap at the foot of her bed, discarded during the night because, thanks to the fire, she had been warm. Deciding that the top could serve her as a short nightshirt, she got out of bed and went to the couch. "Brian! Wake up!" she said urgently. "There's something outside."

A long, pajama-clad arm came out from under the covers. "Come on back to bed," he said happily.

Miranda thrust his arm away. "Get up, you idiot! There's something wrong."

With that, he opened his eyes, looked her over appreciatively in the faint glow of the fire, and repeated his invitation. Then the realization of what she had said seemed to penetrate his consciousness. "What's wrong?" he asked sharply, sitting up.

The harsh scraping could be heard again. "That's it," Miranda said. "That's the sound I heard."

Brian threw his head back and laughed.

"What is it?" Miranda asked, annoyed.

"Come here. I'll show you." He tossed the blanket off and, putting his arm around her slender waist, drew her to the window they had stood at earlier that night. He pulled the curtain aside, and Miranda gasped. The white moonlight spotlighted two deer—a stag with a fine spread of antlers and his doe.

"When they come for their nightly drink of water, they also sharpen their antlers on the rough stone of the cabin. That was the sound you heard." He paused. "They're beautiful, aren't they?"

Miranda could only nod. She had no words to describe how majestically wild yet serene the scene was.

"Were you frightened?" he asked, his arm tightening around her waist.

"Maybe a little," Miranda confessed with a laugh. "You can't help but think of all those horror movies. You know: 'Something was outside in the dark of the lonely Irish countryside—something that wanted in.'"

"Bog Man," Brian said knowingly.

"And *Return of Bog Man,*" Miranda joined in with unaccustomed playfulness.

"I like *Bride of Bog Man* better." His hands loose around her waist now, he turned her toward him and buried his face in her hair. Miranda trembled, excited anew by his closeness. Suddenly, in an explosion of pent-up feeling, he covered her mouth with his, devouring her waiting sweetness. At the same time his hands took possession of her body, caressing her breasts and sides, her warm, naked thighs, and the soft curves of her buttocks.

This time *she* said no to their desire. She stepped away from him and in a low, tense voice said, "I think not, Brian."

"Of course. It's as you wish," he answered hoarsely. "About bogs," he continued in what was obviously an attempt at humor and normalcy, "watch out for them. You'll find them on mountains and in other isolated spots. They're nasty, sticky places, and if you fell in, you might have a hard time getting out."

"I promise to stay out of bogs—scout's honor."

He placed his hand on her neck, under her hair, and Miranda quivered at his touch again. "You must take good care of yourself," he said jokingly. "You belong to me."

"No, I don't, Brian," she answered quietly.

"You don't know it yet, *macushla*, but you're going to marry me."

"Is that more blarney to get around me?"

"I don't need blarney for that." His hand still on her neck, he pulled her toward him and kissed her lightly. "Do I, now?"

During the night, more deer came to drink from the stream and sharpen their antlers on Brian's cabin. Miranda heard them and guessed that Brian did, too. The strain of a man and woman wanting each other made the silence an inaudible scream in the dark.

I won't go through this again, she vowed. Next time, we'll sit at a table on straight chairs—no beds, no couch, no fire . . . no motorcycle, either; no stags and does, and no kisses. But what good is all this when he's probably lying awake over there planning the opposite?

Chapter Five

THE NEXT MORNING, after Brian dropped her off, Miranda unlocked her front door and stopped, key in hand, on the threshold. A forest-green framed backpack, unzipped and spilling female underwear, wrinkled shirts, and a hairbrush, lay on the floor. The acrid smell of burned bacon hung in the air, mingled with—Miranda deduced, sniffing—blackened toast and boiled coffee.

Miranda's lips curved upward in a knowing smile. "Barbara!" she called, starting for the kitchen.

She was met halfway by a young woman with a peaches and cream complexion and short blond hair that framed clever, sharp features. This was Barbara Evans, the English friend with whom Miranda had shared an apartment in Boston when they were both in graduate school. Barbara was a plant geneticist who lived in London and worked at Kew Gardens.

After they had embraced, Barbara drew back and looked at Miranda. "And where have *you* been all night? I got here at nine, and no Miranda. I waited and waited,

and still no Miranda, so I finally went to bed." She waved
a greasy spatula in the air. "Do you want some breakfast?
Or have you already had yours?" she added with a comical leer.

Ignoring her friend's questions and the look that went
with them, Miranda said, "Why didn't you let me know
you were coming? In fact, what are you doing in Killarney?" She looked around—only one backpack and no
male clothes so far as she could see. "Are you alone?"

"Am I ever! I've been traveling with a friend." Barbara raised her blond eyebrows suggestively. "But we
had a big blow-up in Cork, so I came on alone to see
you. I'm really browned off at him, and he knows I'm
here. So if he calls, mum's the word. All right?"

"All right, but I wish you had let me know you were
coming. I could have planned something."

"I did send you a note, along with that printout from
my hiking club about a trip to Scotland next spring."

"But that was ages ago, and the note didn't say *when!*"

Barbara shrugged. "I didn't know. It all depended on
how he and I got on."

"Is this 'he' someone I should meet?"

Barbara laughed. "I shouldn't think so. Colin's fun—
when he's not being medieval about relationships—but
that's as far as it goes." She waved the spatula around
again, and a spot of grease fell on the nylon pack. "You
caught me in the middle of breakfast. I hope you don't
mind my barging in like this and helping myself to things
in your fridge." She looked inquiringly at Miranda as
they walked to the kitchen.

"Don't be absurd; but how did you get in?"

"Miranda, love, a *child* could have found the key
where you put it."

"I always worry about locking myself out," Miranda
answered defensively. "Besides, the last crime in Killarney was probably someone poaching the king's deer."

"I could cook you more bacon," Barbara offered as she sat down to her half-eaten breakfast. "You're out of eggs," she added accusingly.

"Sorry. I'll keep you company, but I don't want anything, thanks."

"Which brings us back to where you were last night," Barbara said with a sidelong humorous glance at Miranda.

"Have you ever heard of Brian O'Bannon?"

"The Irish poet? Of course; he's well known over here. All over the world, I guess. What about him?"

"He's going to be giving a series of lectures at Biochem on poetry and science. I'm helping him with the science part; that's all."

"All night?" Barbara asked incredulously.

Miranda colored. "That was an accident." Vaguely, she waved a hand. "The roads were dark. It would have been dangerous to return to Killarney on his motorcycle." Miranda shrugged. "Besides, nothing happened."

Barbara cast a scathing glance at the plaid skirt and lavender turtleneck. "With *those* clothes, I shouldn't think so."

Accustomed to her friend's bluntness, Miranda simply veered off on a new tack. "Why don't you let me show you around Killarney? I'll take the day off. I'm at a stopping place in my work and have a lot of accumulated vacation time. What do you say?"

"Super! We can gossip and get caught up on the news as we go. Have you heard from the Wolcott Research Institute about the postdoc fellowship you applied for?"

"Not yet, but I expect to soon."

"What will happen to your job here?"

"I took it with the proviso that if the fellowship came through, I could leave with no hard feelings. Walter Royce, my department chief, is a friend of the family and almost like my second father."

"I thought there was only one Frazier Dunn in the pantheon of saintly scientists," Barbara said dryly.

Miranda didn't reply. Her father and Barbara had never hit it off. It had bothered her at first when the English girl had come to her home for Thanksgiving and Christmas and other school holidays, but she had gotten used to their gibes at each other and now ignored them.

Barbara rose and said, "I'll clean up."

"All right, and I'll call the lab and let them know I'm not coming in."

A short while later, when Miranda had gone to her bedroom to dress, Barbara called out from the depths of her backpack, "What are you wearing?"

"Oh, just jeans and a tweed jacket." But the thought that she might meet Brian in town coupled with Barbara's remark about the plaid skirt made her change her mind. "On second thought, I might take you to tea in some spiffy place, so I think I'll wear a dress. Do you have a dress or a skirt?"

"Of course I have a skirt. Do you think I'm a barbarian?"

Standing before the bathroom mirror, applying her makeup while Barbara watched with a critical eye, Miranda listened to her friend's hilarious stories about the men in her life just as she used to when they lived together.

"Hasn't there ever been somebody you wanted to marry?" Miranda asked curiously.

"Never," Barbara said with conviction. "'Meet, mate, and separate,' is my motto. It's more fun that way. There are no emotional hang-ups and no problems. You should try it."

With a decisive shake of her head, Miranda said, "No, that's not for me. I think I would feel cold and empty afterward. What I want is a total relationship comprising sex *and* love."

Barbara shrugged. "Ah, well, you're different from me and always were." She raised a warning finger. "But just watch out while you're looking for that total, committed relationship that you don't end up with another dreary character like your ex."

Miranda raised a rueful eyebrow. "I loved Craig when I married him."

"Did you ever have a good time with him—just ordinary fun, in bed or out?"

Miranda laughed. "Not often."

"That's what I mean," Barbara grumbled.

A familiar *vroom-vroom* vibrated through the air. Miranda flushed and tossed her head and looked in the mirror. At least today he'd be seeing her in clothes that were more her usual style—in this case, a sophisticated cowl-neck sweater-dress in ultramarine blue. Avoiding Barbara's questioning half-smile, Miranda went to the front door and opened it just as the motorcycle engine died to an angry sputter. She ignored the ridiculous flip-flop her heart always performed at the sight of him; she was getting used to *that*. Much more dangerous was the pride she unexpectedly felt.

So what if he's tall and rugged, and his hair is little-boy tousled, and his eyes are a clear, gorgeous blue; you don't own him, for goodness' sake. He's not a possession to be shown off to Barbara, even if you were the type to do that, which you're not.

"Good morning," she called out, coolly cheerful.

"Hello again!" His voice was vibrant with meanings she didn't care to analyze.

She held the door wide. "Come in. To what do I owe the honor?"

"I happened to be at Biochem when you called. Royce mentioned you were taking a friend sightseeing, and I thought I'd offer my services."

Barbara had come up behind them, and with the dazed

expression of an automaton, Miranda introduced Brian.

He was doing it again—moving in on her, taking over her life.

Barbara put her hand out and said, "I've read some of your poetry, Brian. I liked it."

Brian bent his head in a courteous half-bow and answered simply, "Thank you."

Miranda's eyes widened. Flippant Barbara Evans of the casual lifestyle and exponent of shallow relationships read *poetry?* Miranda double-checked for that predatory look she knew so well, but her self-possessed friend seemed completely sincere.

"I heard your offer, Brian," Barbara now said briskly, "and I think it's a good idea to have someone who knows the locale show us around."

"Then it's settled," Brian said. "And I'm to have the company of the two loveliest women in Ireland."

"Do you always go where you're not wanted?" Miranda whispered furiously to him as Barbara returned to the bedroom.

With an injured air, Brian answered, "But I have a feeling that deep down here"—he placed his hand on his heart—"you do want me."

"You're wrong, Brian," Miranda said sweetly, putting her hand on her forehead. "The feeling I have about you is right here, and it's known as a headache."

"What are you two doing, playing charades?" Barbara asked, entering the room again, a scarf of Miranda's tied around her hair. "How about this?" She pointed to her eye, hummed through her lips, and walked briskly to the door.

"I'm going!" Miranda called out.

"Righto," Barbara said, accenting the *o*. "Shall we? I can't go back to Kew without having seen the lakes of Killarney. They're very strong on beauty at Kew, they are."

Driving Miranda's car, Brian first took Miranda and Barbara through the streets of Killarney, past its souvenir shops and small hotels built of pastel-colored stucco and its line of jaunting cars. It was still early enough so that the jarveys, drivers straight out of central casting, with their pipes and caps and old tweeds, were reading the morning paper in the horse-drawn cars. The tourists would come later, to ride through the the countryside—with their feet dangling from wooden seats that faced outward —and listen to the stories the jarveys were famous for.

Brian stopped for a moment by nearby Lough Leane. "That's Innisfallen, that island out there in the middle. It's a beautiful spot. I'd take you there, but it would require a boat and more time than we have today. But you've already seen it, haven't you, Miranda?"

"I'm afraid not. I suppose for no better reason than that I knew I could always go, so I kept putting it off."

"Then you've been depriving yourself of a genuine pleasure," Brian said. "I must take you there some day."

Miranda opened her mouth to protest, but Barbara's amused eye and the now-familiar "it's settled" look on Brian's face stopped her. She sat in the middle of the front seat, between Brian, who was behind the steering wheel on the right, and Barbara on the left-hand passenger side. As they started the popular 112-mile tour of the Iveragh Peninsula that was known as the Ring of Kerry, Miranda felt increasingly as though she and Brian were alone in the car.

It wasn't just their physical closeness—the suspense of almost touching, then his grazing her thigh with his hand as he shifted gears and the bulky feel of his shoulder as she was thrown against him when they rounded a curve. It was also the fact that he spoke only to Barbara, explaining as they went along that the blue-black river that scudded, white-foamed, over jagged black rocks was the Laune, and that the mountains in the distance were

MacGillycuddy's Reeks—*reeks* meaning *rocks,* and MacGillycuddy being the clan that once held the mountain stronghold. It was as though he was saving his silence for Miranda because there were words other than these that he wanted to say to her.

Then Barbara spotted two wild goats perched on a shoulder of land above the river and announced that she wanted a picture of them. Brian stopped the car, and as Barbara walked on ahead toward the buff-colored billies, he put his hand around Miranda's waist to slow her down.

"I haven't had a chance to talk to you alone," he murmured.

"Do we have anything to talk about?" she responded tartly.

"Not all communication is verbal." He drew her into his arms and bent his lips to hers. Wrapped in that close embrace, Miranda felt heady with expectation. *I'm like a chocoholic. I keep saying this one will be the last, but I never can get enough of them.* This kiss had all the freshness of the morning in it, a sweetness that lulled Miranda's senses into joyous acceptance. She let her lips cling to his until a discreet "ahem" nearby made her pull away. A boy in a red jacket, with hair almost as red, was looking away, embarrassed. He was standing beside a donkey with a straw basket on its back, and in the basket sat a brown and white hound, long-eared and mournful-eyed.

"I only wanted to sell ye a bit of heather," the boy said in the up-and-down lilt of the Kerry brogue.

"How much?" Brian asked with a grin, digging into his pocket.

"Whatever ye want to give."

Brian handed the boy some money and accepted a sprig of purple heather. Then the child led the donkey a few steps away, the dog bouncing contentedly in the basket.

Brian fastened the heather in Miranda's blond hair and bent his lips to hers again. "It's an old Irish custom to kiss the girl you pin a bit of heather on," he said.

This time she pushed him away. "Not in front of the goats!"

"More like, not in front of the tourists."

A big tour bus was grinding to a stop behind them. As they watched, a horde of camera-hung, white-haired tourists descended and swarmed around the boy and the donkey.

"Now we know why the kid was out here selling heather," Brian said. "He must hit all the tour buses making a photo stop."

"He probably rents the goats . . ."

"And the dog and donkey." Brian shook his head in wonder. "Anyone who can sell heather in Ireland!"

They were still laughing when Barbara came up to them. "I got some super shots of the river and those goats," she said, beaming with satisfaction. Then she gave Brian and Miranda a long, shrewd assessing look.

They detoured at Killorglin to see Caragh Lake and looked down at the reflection in its still water of mist-shrouded Carrantuohill, the highest peak in Ireland. Then they were on the road that followed the wild coastline, whose eight-hundred-foot cliffs, gold and purple with gorse and heather, towered above the furious, smashing surf of a diamond-bright sea. They continued along Dingle Bay till they came to Rossbeigh Strand, a stretch of golden sand at the foot of green hills, where they got out of the car for more pictures.

Hungry by then, they stopped for lunch at Sneem, a little town of steeply pitched streets with mountains all around it. Brian took them to a pub he knew, a cheerful place with whitewashed walls in the dining room, a fireplace, wooden tables, and red-and-white checked café curtains. The "Pub Grub" special was steak and kidney pie, and they all had that, with Shandies, a mixture of beer and ginger ale, to wash it down.

When, at the end of the meal, Barbara excused herself to take more pictures, Miranda grumbled, "She's only doing that to leave us alone."

"Smart girl, your friend. I like her."

"And I couldn't care less. Do you realize that you don't play a big enough part in my life to either like or dislike my friends? And your pretense in front of Barbara that you have that importance is misleading. I don't want you to look at me all the time or take my hand or kiss me. Your actions are futile. They won't lead anywhere. Believe me, we don't have the kind of relationship you seem to be trying to establish."

It hadn't come out right. She had sputtered and turned pink and hesitated when she had planned to be quite definite and cool. The truth of the matter was, every look and touch and kiss had excited and delighted her immeasurably. But having them witnessed, especially by as astute an observer as Barbara Evans, loaned them an importance, even a permanence, she didn't wish them to have.

However, Brian simply ignored what she'd said. Taking one of her hands in both of his, he laid it across his palm, as if to study it. "Your hands are different from the rest of you. I would have expected long, white tapering fingers to go with your long bones and blondeness. But they're rather small, actually, and blunt, and very capable looking."

As he spoke, he rubbed his thumb meditatively over hers. Then he started to stroke the valleys between her fingers. What he was doing was deliciously arousing and maddening at the same time. He was the most aggravating man! Any situation he couldn't bend to his own purposes he simply bypassed.

"They're my mother's hands," Miranda explained,

wondering even as she did so why she was giving him this personal information. "She's smaller-boned than I and very capable—an avid and accomplished gardener." Miranda laughed. "It's her escape. When Dad gets too much for her, she goes out in her garden and yanks weeds." Feeling disloyal, she added quickly, "Actually, they get along very well. Only, Dad's apt to be a little demanding at times."

"He's an eminent research scientist, I understand."

"Very eminent," Miranda said. "Now may I have my hand back?"

"Of course." But before she could pull it away, he had raised it and brushed his lips across the sensitive skin of her upturned palm.

"I thought I told you I didn't want you to do that."

"Macushla, I know when a woman wants me and when she doesn't," he said gently.

The ripple of arousal that Brian's kiss engendered deepened to a thrill that pulsed throughout her body. It was exciting to think of him as being experienced. Like many newlyweds, she and Craig had been clumsy and unsure with each other. Eventually, they had gotten beyond that stage, but not by much. Love by the clock—between planes and scientific conferences and work schedules—hardly qualified as a garden of delights. For a moment, Miranda's mind toyed with imagining Brian's amorous exploits and wondering what he knew about her that she didn't know herself. Then, impatiently, she turned her thoughts in another direction.

High tea at Killarney's grandest hotel marked the end of the day of sightseeing. Brian took Miranda and Barbara home and, with a casual wave and "a week from Saturday" in response to their shouted "thanks again," roared off on his motorcycle.

"What's going on a week from Saturday?" Miranda asked as she unlocked the front door.

"Brian's taking you and me for a climb up the mountain with a funny name."

"Macgillycuddy's Reeks?"

"The same," Barbara answered, marching purposefully toward the telephone.

"Nobody asked me!" Miranda said hotly.

Barbara's reply was nonchalant. "Brian offered when he heard you and I like to go hiking. There's a note here by the phone. Leprechauns?" she asked.

"My charlady. She has a key and comes and goes pretty much as she pleases."

Barbara looked down at the folded piece of paper in her hand and then, surprised, at Miranda. "It's for me." She opened it and broke into a smile. "All it says is, 'Sorry, Colin,' but wasn't that dear of him?"

"Very," Miranda answered dryly.

Suddenly excited and euphoric, Barbara said, "I'm going back to Cork. I'll take the train. Where's my backpack?"

"I thought you didn't want to see him for a while."

"That was before I traipsed around Killarney with you and your poet. He's bonkers about you, my pet, which reminded me how nice it is to have a man about the house."

"Brian and I aren't living together."

"The more fool *you*." Barbara shot her friend a pitying glance and walked into the bedroom.

Chapter Six

THE FIRST POETRY and science lecture was only a week away, and several more evenings of preparation were required. Nothing was less romantic than a kitchen, Miranda decided, so at her insistence, she and Brian ended up working at her shiny Formica and chrome table by the gas stove. Miranda wore her plaid skirt and a plain blouse and ignored Brian's raised eyebrow and frown. She served black coffee, and a prosaic electric fire glowed in the living room grate.

Their last session took place on Saturday morning, and the weather was sunny and dry for a change. They were just winding up their work when Janet Royce telephoned. "Miranda! There's not a cloud in the sky. If you and Brian have finished your business, why don't the two of you come play doubles with Walter and me."

Miranda's eyes sparkled at the thought of tennis. She loved the clean thump of the ball against the court, the lightning-swift follow-through, and the exciting challenge of the game.

"Brian," she called out from the living room, "it's Janet Royce. Do you want to play tennis?"

"Yes, fine," he called back.

"I heard all that," Janet said on the phone. "Brian's racket and shoes are at our place. Tell him we'll bring them. Meet you at the courts in fifteen minutes?"

"Yes, we'll be there. It will only take me a minute to change, and Brian has his motorcycle."

Brian's brilliant blue eyes glowed with happiness as he lifted Miranda onto the rear seat of his motorbike. After he mounted, he tucked her arms around him. The tide of contentment that flowed through Miranda as she settled her body against his prompted her to lay her head for one brief moment against Brian's broad back. It felt so good to be practically wrapped around him again, almost to have him in her arms, to feel his hard, muscular back against her soft breasts. If life were only entirely physical, how easy it would be, she mused.

The tennis courts were behind the Biochem buildings, and the Royces were already there, rallying. Janet gave Brian a warm, motherly smile as she handed him his racquet.

Walter slung a pair of laced tennis shoes around Brian's neck and slapped him on the back. "Hurry up, Brian. Janet and I are hot today. We're going to beat the pants off you kids."

And so, to Miranda's chagrin, they did. She had never played with Brian, but she had watched him and he was good. Today, however, he was definitely off his game. When it was his serve, he double-faulted. Forehand drives sputtered into errors, forehand volleys sailed, and approach shots landed soft and short. Miranda didn't play much better than Brian, and so it went until they were shaking hands and congratulating the Royces and accepting an invitation to their home for lunch.

As they walked back to where Brian had left his motorcycle, his happy-go-lucky expression, his obvious *happiness,* nettled Miranda.

"Don't you even care that we lost?" she asked.

"No, why should I? It's only a game."

"Of course it's only a game, but it's a game one plays to win."

"Do *you* feel badly that we lost?"

"Yes, I don't believe in losing. It could get to be a habit."

He stopped and looked at her in amazement. "Is that how you look at life—always in terms of winning or losing?"

Miranda bit her lower lip. She didn't like being put on the defensive. But suddenly it was important to her that he know her and what had made her that way.

"When I was a little girl, I often didn't want to do my homework because I preferred to stay outside and play; when I was older, I got in with a wild bunch in high school and neglected my school work for a while, and in college I wanted to take a year off and travel around Europe. Each time, my father asked, 'Do you want to be a winner or a loser, Miranda? The choice is yours.' Put like that, there was never a question in my mind about what was the right thing for me to do. I still feel the same way. I don't intend ever to lose, if I can help it."

Brian chuckled. "It certainly simplifies life, and it's highly applicable to tennis."

"But poets are above such crassness, I suppose."

"It's hard to win or lose a poem," Brian said meditatively.

And that's what makes poetry unimportant, Miranda reflected.

Brian passed his hand under her thick hair and rested it lightly on her neck. "Life isn't a matter of climbing ladders, Miranda. It's the exploring of marvelously intricate and complex labyrinths."

Miranda shook her head loose from his grasp. "Maybe to you it is, but I don't see it that way."

She felt cross and unhappy, ashamed of making such a big deal out of losing a tennis game and of telling that childish anecdote about herself. But when she put her arms around Brian's firm waist again and the motorcycle carried them away into a private world of air and motion, a wellspring of mingled happiness and desire surged up within her. She wanted to run her hands over him, to feel every inch of the muscle and sinew and flesh that were his; to slip her hand under his shirt and lay it against his skin; to trace the line of the strong thighs that gripped the sides of the motorcycle. Most of all, she wanted him to kiss her and hold her in his arms. She wanted very much to go to bed with Brian O'Bannon.

But she was not Barbara Evans. Without love, no relationship was possible, and how could she love a man so different from her? Love implied at least a modicum of companionship. Brian and she couldn't even play tennis together! And she could just see her father's face if she said, "I'm going to marry a poet, Dad."

Let's face it, Miranda, you like the guy and you're attracted to him, but you're not in love with him. Once these damn lectures are over, you can write finish *to this little chapter in your life.*

As Brian lifted her off the motorcycle in front of the Royces' house, holding her longer than was necessary, Miranda saw Janet Royce watching from a window.

"You and Brian make a handsome couple," Janet said later, when she and Miranda were alone in the kitchen. "Brian's a wonderful person. Walter and I are very fond of him."

"Are you matchmaking, Janet?" Miranda asked in surprise, remembering how Janet had all but warned her off Brian at the Royces' party after the poetry reading.

But Janet spoke now as if she had forgotten her previous opinion. "You could do worse, much worse. Brian's an absolutely charming man and so handsome and... and... sexy."

Miranda's lips curved into a smile. Casual references to sex still seemed daring to women like Janet and Miranda's mother.

"I thought you wanted me to marry a scientist," Miranda said, tongue in cheek.

"That was before I got used to seeing you and Brian as a couple. I thought, because you were so wrapped up in your work, that only another scientist could interest you. But being with Brian seems to have changed you. You've become looser, freer, happier somehow. And I know from marriages I've observed that comrades in the laboratory sometimes turn out to be very cool colleagues in the bedroom." Janet Royce thereupon pressed her small lips together firmly and marched out of the kitchen.

Miranda stood for a moment, nonplussed. Walter was fishing regularly in Brian's salmon stream. One could hardly be invited out anywhere in Yanktown without meeting the popular Irish poet. And here her Aunt Janet, who had been pushing every unmarried Biochem research fellow at Miranda since she arrived in Ireland, had not only just described Miranda's marriage in a nutshell but was actually promoting Brian O'Bannon's sexy qualities!

"It's hard for a girl to stay virtuous," she said aloud in simpering Cockney.

"Is it virtuous you want to be?" Brian said from behind her. "Then you have to practice struggling against temptation, my beauty. What would you do if a man put his arms around you like this?" Miranda laughed as she felt his strong arms encircle her and pull her lithe, supple body against his. "Suppose the blackguard tried to steal a kiss?" With tantalizing slowness, he slid his hands across her breasts and turned her around so that she faced him. Her heart beating a mad tattoo, she let him take her lips in a long, achingly sweet kiss.

"You didn't struggle," he said in a low voice, when he finally let her go.

"Next time," she whispered.

He swept his lips across her cheekbone, then buried his face in her hair. "I want you so much, Miranda. I love the way you move, slender and graceful and precise as a gazelle, and the way you stand, so silent and thoughtful, your dark eyes drinking things in like deep wells." He bit her ear, then gave it a healing lick with the tip of his tongue, although the gentle pressure of his teeth hadn't hurt. Rather, the little love bite had sent an erotic surge of excitement through her. "And I know you want me," he said seductively. "Life isn't a dress rehearsal, *macushla*. When will you let us love each other?"

"It's because it isn't a dress rehearsal that I can't make a mistake," she answered, reluctantly pulling herself out of his embrace.

"Afraid of piling up zeroes on that great big scorecard of life?" he said tauntingly.

"Yes, if you must know the truth."

A restless, vaguely unhappy feeling took hold of Miranda when she got home. Only work seemed to assuage it, so she spent the next day washing everything possible—her hair, the car, the kitchen floor, and all the windows in her house.

Early Monday morning, she was at her workbench, carrying out experiments that would test the ability of certain pathogenic organisms to produce mutants resistant to a new antibiotic. But the puzzle-solving she did in her lab was a piece of cake compared to the problem Brian O'Bannon presented. *If you can't love him, leave him, Miranda. Oh, sure; you try it, Miss Cool.*

* * *

That night, the first of the poetry and science lectures, found Miranda on tenterhooks with nervousness for Brian, and it didn't help to tell herself that it was only because she had had a hand in formulating the lectures. The minute he walked out onto the podium, dressed in his green Donegal tweed jacket and flyaway tie, his handsome face wind-reddened from the ride on his motorbike and his hair glossy with brushing, she felt a definite pang of proprietary interest. That's your man up there, a voice within insisted. Start pulling for him.

But never did a speaker need less help than Brian O'Bannon. Cogently and logically, he showed, through his reading and discussion of certain poems, that a poem met many of the criteria for a living organism. Its pattern was an orderly structural arrangement, one, moreover, that continued to grow like a biological entity as more of its meanings were discovered. A poem had purposiveness. As birds built nests to house their young, so poets constructed poems to convey ideas and emotions. A poem was an information system depending on the order of its words, as genetic information was an orderliness implicit in the structure of nucleic-acid molecules. He pointed out, too, that the excitement of exploring a poem was similar to the excitement of discovery in a research laboratory.

Brian asked for questions at the end of his talk, and proof of the interest he had aroused was evident in the number of hands that went up. His questioners were highly intelligent, trained people, and Miranda appreciated the tact with which he made his explanations. She also liked the care he took to express his ideas precisely. Seeing the earnestness with which he addressed himself to each question, she realized his seriousness of purpose as a poet. It was evident that to him leisure activities like tennis were really only games; poetry was important. Miranda's eyes shone with admiration. His nonchalant attitude toward conventional games was really a sign of independence. Brian could go along with the crowd without slavishly following it.

At the second poetry and science lecture on Wednesday night, Brian invited his audience to try their hand at writing a poem. To her chagrin, Miranda couldn't even start. She took the blank piece of paper home with her, then angrily crumpled it up and threw it away. Moreover, although she usually enjoyed the easy repartee of the lab, she found that when her colleagues discussed poetry she was unable, because of some obscure inhibition, to formulate even a comment.

She was beginning to hate poetry, but she didn't know why. Her antipathy to it was one of life's unsolved problems. She had been lucky so far; there hadn't been many. Only your marriage, she told herself wryly. And if there was a connection, for the life of her she couldn't see it.

On Friday night, the third and last lecture drew the biggest crowd of all. In the question-and-answer period that followed Brian's talk, driven by some compulsion she didn't fully understand, Miranda raised her hand. She reddened slightly at the tender look in Brian's eyes and the soft way he said, "Yes, Miss Dunn?" there in front of an auditorium full of people, but she plunged on.

"I agree with you, Mr. O'Bannon, that scientists bring to their reading of literature the virtues of logical habits of thought, insistence upon demonstration, and precision of approach, but isn't there an enormous difference between science and literature in that there are objective standards in science and none in literature? You know what I mean, I'm sure. Certain authors are 'in' for a while, then their popularity fades; eventually they're revived, only to die out again. That kind of faddishness doesn't occur in science. Boyle's Law is always Boyle's Law."

"No one, I think, would be fool enough to say that poetry and science are identical," Brian began in the tone of gentle reproof one would use with a child. "I was merely searching out the similarities between what seem at first to be two very dissimilar endeavors—literature and science." Then, his eyes gleaming with suppressed laughter, he thrust his hands in his pockets and rocked on his heels. "And although I wouldn't presume to criticize science, Boyle having been an Irishman and all, wasn't it Freud's belief that depression was anger turned inward, whereas now, only some decades later, scientists are looking for genes that cause this state?"

The auditorium rocked with laughter, but Miranda sat stony-faced, staring straight ahead of her. She was furious that he would descend to such a cheap trick as playing to the audience for laughs. She resented his belittling of her and was even shocked by it. She had thought him too sensitive a person for that kind of behavior, but evidently she had been wrong. Unwilling to cause a scene, she sat on, blotting out the sight of Brian and the sound of his voice, until the program was over. Then she stood up, belted her raincoat tightly about her, and walked out.

Tomorrow was the day Brian had invited her to climb Macgillycuddy's Reeks. Miranda decided that she would call him in the morning and call off the expedition, which was only tentative anyway. She told herself that it was a relief finally to have a reason not to see him.

In spite of her agitation, Miranda fell asleep almost as soon as she went to bed, but at four o'clock she was wide awake. She got up and stood by the window. It was within a half hour of dawn. The fresh morning breeze didn't have the dampness of rain, and it occurred to her to climb MacGillycuddy's Reeks by herself. She was a fairly experienced climber, and what a welcome change it would be to shift from the muddle of relationships to the clear-cut challenge of climbing a mountain.

The sun was just touching Lough Leane when Miranda took a canvas bag she kept in the garage and put some cheese and bread and a plastic bottle of water in it and started off. Retracing the route Brian had taken, she drove to the base of Macgillycuddy's Reeks. The top was still hidden by mist, but she had no intention of climbing that far anyway. All she planned to do was hike until she was tired, stop for lunch, and then return to Killarney.

Taking a large-scale map of the Killarney district out of her bag and sticking it in her pocket, Miranda began to climb. At first, the going was easy. There were no marked trails as such, but there were bootprints to follow and little piles of stones that marked the route. She was on rising grassland where she passed flocks of black-faced sheep and occasionally met a shepherd in brown corduroys and the rubber boots called Wellingtons.

The sparkling air and sunlight were healing her spirit. Soon Miranda wasn't thinking of Brian but only of putting one foot in front of the other, and she was glad she had come. She ate her lunch on a large flat rock where the only sound was the wind whistling in the heather. Sitting alone at what seemed like the edge of the world, she found herself thinking of Brian again and wishing he were beside her. He'd be a good climbing companion, with his strength and easygoing way and sense of humor. But she pushed the fugitive thought away, telling herself impatiently that he would probably spout poetry up here on the mountain and she'd have to listen to it.

Recalling his humiliation of her at the final poetry and science lecture, she felt spurred to show she could climb the Reeks without him; so she rose and pushed on instead of turning back as she had intended. The heather and yellow gorse soon gave way to steep rock that was much harder to climb—and therefore more fun to try, she assured herself. Then she reached a plateau like the one where she had stopped for lunch and decided that the climb had been worthwhile. She could see miles of ocean and coastline all the way to Bantry Bay. And on the eastern side, the land flowed away like emerald velour until it concealed itself in a blue haze.

The sun was low now, and it was obvious that she wouldn't make it back to Killarney before nightfall. But Miranda wasn't perturbed. On the way up, she had noticed a shepherd's hut—a shaggy little building of rough dry-stone walls with grass growing between the stones. She would spend the night there. She had the heel of her loaf of bread and a piece of yellow cheese left, and some water.

She climbed down the rock without difficulty, and when she reached the first plateau she started looking for the hut. But every familiar-looking narrow dirt trail that she followed seemed to peter out on the empty mountainside. Miranda realized then that she had come too far west and was still high above the hut. But night was falling, and a mountain was no place to tramp around after dark. So she walked a short distance farther till she found some soft bracken to lie on and, putting her canvas bag under her head, tried to sleep. But even her anorak and corduroy jeans couldn't keep out the damp, bone-biting cold.

After a while, she stood up, stamping her numb feet and beating her arms across her chest to keep warm. To ward off sleep, she started walking in ever-widening circles. She had just taken a step when suddenly the earth felt soft under her feet. Alarmed, she tried to retreat but it was no good. The ground gave way like a wet sponge. Water sucked at her knees, was cold against her thighs. It seeped through her jeans and even her jacket. The stink of leaf mold made her cough, a sharp explosion of sound in the utter silence.

The gates of panic stood wide open. The stench of the bog, the dark and the loneliness and danger threatened to overwhelm her self-control. But if ever she needed a clear head and command of every movement, it was now, because she was sinking faster than she would have thought possible.

Slowly, she felt with her hands for tussocks of grass. Careful as she was, her movements caused the cold slimy water to squelch up in her face. But there were stable tufts of grass within reach. If she could grasp them and they didn't break off in her hands, she would stand a chance.

Miranda tested each grass clump; then, putting all her strength into her arms and shoulders, she both pulled and heaved herself out of the bog. She felt the bracken under her springy and alive, not pulpy with decay. She started to shake with relief; then tears came, bringing total release of her emotions. Purged of shock and fear, she was able to think again. Even now, she was not out of danger. A single false step could send her into the bog again.

So she lay there, tense-limbed and racked with cold, and recited chemical formulas to keep herself awake until dawn. But she must have dozed off, because the light she saw swinging from side to side in a golden nimbus made her think first of fairies and then of the will-o'-the-wisp that leads travelers astray. Something cold and wet touched her face. Whatever it was, it soon ceased. And from not so far away as a dream would have it, she heard a man's voice shouting "Hullo! Hullo!"

It's Brian . . . Brian who knows every inch of Macgillycuddy's Reeks and who was going to come with me today. And Brian has a dog with him. And I'm going to be rescued!

"Brian! I'm over here. But there's a bog very close. I'm on the edge of it."

"Keep calling, Miranda. The dog will find you. Are you all right?"

"Yes," she called back. Then the dog was there, nudging her side. The broad golden arcs of the light were coming closer. At first, the big, burly figure was shadowy and Miranda felt a stab of fear. Then it was Brian, lifting her up and holding her against him.

And suddenly the awfulness of the black night and the terror of sinking into the soft, gluey marsh overcame her. She buried her face in his shoulder and cried again.

He stroked her hair rhythmically and crooned, "Ssh, *macushla*, it's all right. You're all right now."

"Damn bog!" she said when she had reached the sniffing stage. "There's a shepherd's hut around here somewhere, but I couldn't find it."

"I know where it is, and with the dog and my torch we won't have any trouble finding it. Can you walk?"

"Of course I can walk. It was shock—not self-pity—that made me cry on your shoulder just now."

Brian laughed. "Perhaps you'd rather I didn't rescue you."

"No, you can rescue me," Miranda grumbled. "But you'd better be fast about it. My teeth are making this place sound like a graveyard on Halloween."

With the brown and white foxhound going in front and Brian gripping Miranda's arm, they made their way about a quarter of a mile down the steep slope.

"Here it is," Brian said. He kicked open the weathered wooden door and placed his large flashlight on the dirt floor.

Miranda looked down at herself in the light. Her clothes were covered with mud and bog slime. She pulled bits of bracken and grass out of her hair. A scratch on her face was bleeding. But worst of all was the cold. She was shivering uncontrollably.

"You're going to be sick if you don't get out of those clothes," Brian said flatly. "The shepherds always leave some peat for each other for a fire. I'll start one right away."

Shivering, she stood and watched him work at getting

a fire going in a crude stone fireplace. When the first orange glow appeared, she moved close to it. "What made you come?" she asked.

"It would make more sense to ask how I could not come. I was pretty angry that you took off without either breaking or confirming our date. I guessed you had decided to climb the Reeks alone when I saw your canvas trail bag and water bottle were missing from the shelf in your garage, which, by the way, you neglected to lock. I borrowed the dog, a good tracker, from a fox-hunting friend, and gave him a handkerchief that you had left at the Royces. All this took time, so I got a late start; but I'm damn glad I came. Don't you know better than to go climbing alone? What if you had fallen and broken something, or hadn't gotten out of that bog?"

"I'm an experienced climber," she said weakly.

"Experience can't cover all eventualities," Brian muttered. He wrinkled his nose. "Also, I hate to say this, love, but you give off a definite aroma."

"I know. Canal Number Five."

Brian coughed discreetly at the bad joke, or maybe the bog stench that rose from her clothes was getting to him, Miranda thought. The sound of her teeth going like castanets all night might be bearable, but smelling her wouldn't be.

"I'm going to strip," she said succinctly, "before we're both asphyxiated." She looked around at the bare hut. "But how? I mean, with modesty."

Brian's face took on a wicked look of amusement. "You're sure about that? The modesty, I mean."

"I'm sure," she replied emphatically.

Brian sighed. "Well, in that case." He looked down at his green nylon parka. It was midthigh on him, had two breast pockets and two handwarmer pockets, and a hood. He undid the row of brass snaps on the storm flap, then unzipped the jacket.

"I seem to spend most of my time extricating you

from mud holes and lending you my clothes," he grumbled. He looked at the jacket again. "This would cover you," he said, "but it's only a nylon shell. It would be pretty uncomfortable with nothing underneath it."

With that, he peeled off the white turtleneck he wore under the jacket and handed it to her. Miranda took it wordlessly, her eyes fixed on his broad shoulders and massive chest furred with black hair. Suddenly, his maleness seemed overwhelming; Miranda hesitated, one hand holding his sweater, the other stopped at the top of her jacket zipper. Then a racking shiver broke the impasse.

"Turn your back, please," she said quietly, then started to undress, throwing each piece of clothing to the ground as she removed it.

When she slid the turtleneck over her head and smoothed it down to her knees, she felt as though the garment, still warm with Brian's body heat, created a physical intimacy with him. She savored the feel of it against her bare skin. On the other hand, large though the knit was, it was definitely molding itself to her shape. Jerking it down like a window shade only increased its clinging qualities. And pulling it out away from her at the sides seemed to make it snap back over her breasts and hips like a rubber band.

A mischievous gleam lit Brian's eyes. He had put his jacket on again, and as Miranda's glance fell on it, he said, "No, Miranda, not the jacket, too. I've given you all I'm going to tonight"—he paused dramatically—"in the way of clothing." Then he took a step toward her. "But are you warm enough?" he asked, his tone full of solicitude.

"Yes, thanks. I'll just stay in front of the fire." It was giving off enough heat now to stop the chattering of her teeth and was filling the hut with its own pungent smell.

"All night?"

"Do you have another idea?" she asked, pointedly

surveying the empty hut and dirt floor.

Brian pulled what looked like a large Boy Scout knife out of his pocket. "I think I can gather enough vegetation outside to make us some kind of bed. Which do you prefer, double or king?" he inquired brightly.

"Twin, and nothing else but."

"I'm not sure there's enough foliage out there for *that*, my love." He picked up the flashlight. "Can you get along without this for a while?"

"I have the fire," she answered.

"Right. Well, I shouldn't be long. I'm leaving McGonigle to guard you."

"McGonigle?"

"The foxhound outside. I named him for his owner, and since McGonigle's not around to object . . . by the way, I've got some antiseptic for that scratch on your cheek. Shall I put it on?"

Miranda's hand went to her face. "No, it's all right, thanks." Only after he had gone did she think she should have taken the antiseptic.

A short while later, he returned with an armful of bracken and dropped it at her feet. "Here, you can arrange this lot for yourself. I'll go get more. You'll have your twin beds after all."

Miranda was bending over the dry ferns and grasses, forming them into an elongated, rectangular shape, when she became aware that Brian had returned and was standing in the doorway watching her. She straightened up and faced him, conscious that the fire behind her outlined her shape inside the long knit garment, that her feet were bare, her face scratched, and her hair disheveled.

"Just call me nature girl," she said with a laugh.

He didn't answer, but his eyes never left her as he let the bundle of grasses he was holding fall to the floor and put the flashlight down. "Do you want the antiseptic?" he asked quietly. She nodded, and he walked toward her.

"Shall I put it on, then?" he murmured, and she whispered, "Yes."

The touch of his fingers as he applied the cool antiseptic cream to her fire-heated face sent a frisson of arousal down her spine. He mistook the movement and put a hand on her shoulder to steady her. "Does it sting?" he asked.

"Not much."

They were so close now that their shadows, huge on the wall, looked like one. His hand left her cheek and gripped her lightly under the chin, holding her face tilted up to him. And when his mouth covered hers, twisting against it, devouring it with his own hungry need, she felt everything that was resistant in her dissolve. I'm a candle, she thought, burning and melting at one time.

His arms swept around her and her breasts strained against the white turtleneck, seeking his caress. With sensuous slowness, he stroked each soft sphere until she could feel the pink seed at its tip flower under his fingers. Then he bent his head and pulled at the bud with his teeth, moving the knit material lightly back and forth across it, tantalizing her nerve ends with longing. The firelight caught his face, and the expression of raw desire on it made Miranda tremble with her need for him. It must have been like this with the cavemen, she thought, and her passion rose in crescendos as his hands and mouth pleasured her.

As his lips took hers again, she undid the metal snaps of his parka. "Miranda!" he sighed hoarsely. His tongue glided silkily inside her waiting mouth, caressing its moist interior. When her hand was on the zipper that still held his parka together, his own impatient hand helped her. Then his flesh was hers, and she placed the backs of her hands over the smooth surface of his flat stomach to feel its resilient warmth.

"Why did you give me a hard time at the lecture?"

she whispered, still faintly resentful.

"Is that why you didn't call me and went climbing the Reeks alone?"

She didn't answer. Even now she wouldn't give him the satisfaction of knowing how much he had come to mean to her.

His large hands gripped her sides, their thumbs splayed across her yearning breasts. "It was *you* who gave *me* a hard time, Miranda, with that snide question. But I don't care about that." His hold tightened. "When I think that I almost lost you," he murmured, his voice tight with emotion. "You must never do such a foolhardy thing again." He gave her a little shake. "Do you promise, *macushla?*"

"I'm responsible for my own life, Brian. I can't promise someone else that I will take care of it."

He laughed, and she thought he looked like a pirate with his black hair and tanned face and teeth gleaming in the firelight. "You're a stubborn woman, Miranda. I think if I asked you to stay in the hut, you'd go out. Or if I asked you to go out, you'd stay."

Suddenly, without warning, he pulled her down with him on the bed of dried bracken. He held her tight in his arms, his blue eyes snapping with glee. "And if I said, 'Come to bed,' you wouldn't, much as you wanted to," he continued seductively, his breath warm against her hair and in her ear.

"You make a lot of assumptions, don't you?" Miranda said.

Brian grinned wickedly. "It's known as poetic license."

His mood abruptly changed then. A look of fervid longing crossed his face. He poised himself above her, and his mouth came down with hard, driving force on hers. She met his passion with her own, reaching upward for his burning kiss and threading her fingers through the glorious dark mat on his chest. His hand smoothed its way up her leg under the long sweater, and she stretched out under him like a cat, letting the ripples of longing that his caress created flow through her.

Then, suddenly, his hand was no longer there. His lips slowly left hers, and he sat up. His face, moody and unhappy, was turned to the fire. A long shudder racked his frame and he clenched his fists.

Still not looking at her, he said in a voice shaking despite a visible effort at control, "Much as I want you, *macushla,* and it's killing me to want you the way I do, I'll wait until I have your love." He got up abruptly. "And so help me God, Miranda, you're the only woman I've ever felt that way about."

He made up a bed then of the bracken he had dropped by the door. It was not far from her own makeshift bed, because he needed the heat of the fire, but he resolutely lay down with his back to her.

Miranda lay with her hands folded behind her head for a long time. The torment of longing she felt for the man lying so close gradually left her, but the torment of her mind didn't. Every road she might walk with Brian seemed to be blocked. He was an Irish poet; she was an American scientist. Their worlds weren't even contiguous except for this single, isolated period of his lectures at Biochem. Then there was poetry itself—that emotional dredging of the soul. She wanted no part of it; didn't want to get involved with it; didn't even like it.

Why not? asked that still, small voice of honesty. Why do you get so upset whenever the subject comes up? Why can't you discuss it, debate it, or even try your hand at writing a poem?

Or was it the poet, or marriage, or even men? Brian had said in one of his lectures that the play impulse was central to poetry as it was to all creative endeavors, even science. There had been precious little playing in her

marriage to Craig. Was that what had caused it to foun-
der? Whose fault had it been—hers or Craig's, or both
of theirs? Would her failure with Craig be repeated with
Brian?

Miranda was exhausted and sleep came quickly. Her
last conscious thought was, I'll think about it tomorrow.
If I can't love Brian, I'll give him up.

Chapter Seven

IT WAS BARELY light when Miranda woke up. She was cold and unconsciously reached to pull a blanket up. When her hand fell on the rough grasses that partly covered her, she remembered where she was and sat up.

Brian was at the crude little fireplace, stooped over. As Miranda rustled around in the makeshift bed, he straightened up and turned to face her. "Mornin', darlin'," he said with a grin. "Sleep well?"

"Like the proverbial rock. I'm cold as one, too. Are you building a fire?"

"I can't. We used all the peat last night, except for the small amount I'm obligated to leave for the next fellow. I suggest we get going right away. We'll drop the dog at McGonigle's, then I'll take you home."

"On your motorcycle?" Miranda had a picture of herself holding a squirming foxhound in her arms and didn't like it.

Brian shook his head. "Not knowing in what condition I'd find you, I borrowed McGonigle's van and left my motorbike at his farm." Brian pointed to the parka. "McGonigle insisted that I take his jacket, too, for warmth and to save my own. Your anorak and jeans are dry, and I brushed most of the mud off. There's still a certain lingering aroma about them, but they'll do so long as you stay outdoors," he added with a chuckle.

Although the mountain was still shrouded in a gray, gauzy mist when they started out, the descent was easy and fast. As Miranda had surmised, Brian was a good climber. Moreover, he knew several shortcuts. What Miranda didn't expect was her emotional reaction when they reached her car.

"There were moments back there when I really thought I wouldn't make it," she said, choking up as she looked around her at the road and fields. "But I'm here after all, thanks to you."

"Thanks to your own courage and good sense." Brian's voice was gruff with emotion. In a lighter tone, he said, "Even so, I don't think you're quite ready yet to drive. If you'll give me the keys, I'll have one of McGonigle's lads fetch the car and bring it to the farm while we're still there. I'd drive it, but I don't want to deprive McGonigle of his van any longer than necessary."

Miranda hesitated. It was not her way to cave in under adverse physical conditions. She certainly could drive if she had to; but the cold seemed to have settled in her bones, she was sorely in need of food, and her body ached from sleeping on the ground. So she took her car keys out of the pocket of her anorak and handed them to Brian. "These McGonigles must be very good friends of yours," Miranda said as Brian helped her up into the cab of McGonigle's "van," which turned out to be a pickup, and whistled the foxhound into the back of the small truck.

"They are *that*," Brian answered humorously. "I used to work for Tim McGonigle on the farm when I was a poor, starving poet. Tim and Maureen are grand people. Not only are we friends, but I've been godfather, courtesy uncle, fishing instructor, soccer coach, and dancing master to their kids throughout the years. I've also changed a nappie or two in my time. And if you're thinking I'm sounding like a frustrated father, you're quite right."

"Then why didn't you marry? I'm sure *some* woman would have had you," she said acerbically.

His lips lifted in a half-smile as he briefly took his eyes from the road and looked her over in a way that made her breathless with suspense. "It's not just a wife-mother and children I want, *macushla*. I want a woman for myself, as well."

Miranda was silent, thinking. Craig and she had agreed to put off having children until both were better established in their careers; then they had divorced. If she married again, this time there would be no delay. At twenty-nine, she had to be careful that her best child-bearing years didn't pass her by. As for combining motherhood and work—it wouldn't say much for her competence as a woman or a scientist if she couldn't handle both, Miranda decided.

Soon they were at the McGonigles'. At the familiar sound of the motor, a troop of angel-faced, blue-eyed children came pouring out of the house to greet Brian and look Miranda over and order the foxhound out of the pickup. They were followed by a tall, buxom woman in her forties with humorous blue eyes and a strong jaw.

This was Maureen McGonigle, who interrupted Brian's story of the bog rescue with a stern, "Whatever are you thinking of, Brian O'Bannon, to keep Miranda out here shivering? You must have breakfast with us, but first I'll have one of the girls draw you a warm bath, Miranda." She looked Miranda over. "You're Delia's size, I should think. Delia!" she called to a slim girl of about eighteen, evidently the oldest in the family. "Will you get one of your best outfits for Miss Dunn to wear?" Turning to Miranda again, she said, "I'll wash your bog-stained clothes and send them to you by Brian."

Miranda knew better than to refuse. She had already encountered so many instances of generosity from the Irish people that she knew Maureen would be hurt if she didn't accept her offer.

A short while later, Miranda was soaking away the aches of the night in a gloriously warm tub. Only the smell of bacon frying got her out of the water. She was ravenous and, taking a towel from the heated rack in the large bathroom, quickly patted herself dry. Delia had laid out a soft green woolen turtleneck and a forest-green corduroy skirt as well as some underwear for her. Miranda dressed and looked at herself in a mirror. Only the shoes she had on were hers. Brian had washed them well, then put a heated stone in each to dry them without cracking the leather.

"The clothes become you, miss," Delia said when, after a discreet knock, she entered her own bedroom.

"Please call me Miranda. I would want you to anyway, but now that I'm wearing your clothes..." Miranda's gaze returned to the mirror. "It's amazing, I never thought I looked good in green."

"It's your light hair and fair skin," Delia said matter-of-factly. "They're my good-luck clothes," she continued with a shy smile. "I was wearing them when my boyfriend proposed." She proudly extended her left hand to show a small but pretty diamond.

"When's the happy day going to be?"

"Oh, not till Mike receives a rise in salary. He's just starting out in a chartered accountant's office in Cork. We'd best go down to breakfast now," she said, walking to the door. "That's what I came up to tell you."

Looking at the young woman's glowing face as she stood waiting by the door, Miranda asked impulsively, "How did you know?"

"Know?" Delia repeated, a puzzled look in her eyes.

"That you loved him." Miranda regretted the question the moment she asked it. She'd get some silly teenage answer or intimate details she didn't want to hear or, worse, an invitation to a "heart-to-heart."

But Delia fixed her with serious eyes. "I didn't, for the longest time. And it was torture in a way—not knowing—because I like things clean-cut and definite. Then it came over me in a rush like, one evening when we went to the pictures and ended up afterward at a *ceili.*"

"What's a *ceili?*" Miranda asked, giving the word Delia's pronunciation—*kay-lee.*

"It's a program of traditional Irish dancing, something like your American square dances. Well, the fiddles were scraping away at 'The Walls of Limerick' and I looked at Mike, with his ginger hair flopping all over his face and his lower lip stuck out the way it does when he gets stubborn, except this time he was concentrating on keeping the steps straight—and I knew. And I never asked myself again, did I love him."

Just then Maureen McGonigle called from the foot of the stairs, "Delia! Miranda! I won't hold this bacon a minute longer!"

Breakfast was a magnificent spread of orange juice and porridge, called stirabout, to start, followed by thick slabs of bacon, two kinds of sausage, and ham—all from the same McGonigle pig—eggs from the farm's own hens, brown soda bread and scones with fresh butter, blackberry jam from berries picked by the children that summer, and tea so strong, Miranda had to cut it with hot water and then milk before she could drink it.

Her glance kept drifting to Brian, again clothed in his white turtleneck and his own tweed jacket. His hair was still damp from his bath or shower, and it curled in the most delectable way around his ears. He was obviously a favorite of the household. The children vied for his attention or asked to be excused for a moment to fetch something—a prize essay, a new game, or a stamp collection—they wanted to show him. Maureen kept passing him dishes, and Delia talked to him seriously about Mike's opportunities in Cork. The thought occurred to Miranda that these were his people—that he could never leave them, and that she could never stay. Then she reminded herself that this was not a problem she need worry about; their relationship hadn't and never would reach that point.

And yet his eyes kept pulling her inside the warm, cozy circle he and the McGonigles made, and Miranda knew it wasn't mere politeness. He wanted to make her part of his life. But she, Miranda Dunn, couldn't "know" in a flash, as Delia had. She had to analyze and think logically and objectively. It was what she had been trained for, what she believed in, what she was good at.

As Miranda stood at the door, thanking Maureen for breakfast and patting assorted children on the head, Delia came up to her with a thick, creamy crewneck pullover in her hands.

"It's still misty out, Miranda. Take my jumper, why don't you?"

Looking down at the heavy, almost sculptured hand-knit sweater with its intricate pattern of stitches, Miranda said instinctively, "Oh, no, it's too lovely."

"Not at all. Keep it as long as you like. Do you know what the stitches stand for?" Miranda shook her head. "Years ago every fishing community on the Aran Islands, where this was made, had its own pattern of stitches so that the men could be identified by their hometown should they perish at sea, poor souls. The cable is for the fishing ropes"—Delia pointed to the row of cable stitches down the center of the sweater—"the diamonds for the nets, and the trellis for the little fields with the stone fences around them."

To please Delia, Miranda slipped the sweater on, tumbling her hair as she did so until it swung in a pale golden cloud around her face. Later, when they were in her car, which two of the McGonigle boys had brought to the farm and Brian was now driving, Miranda looked down at her borrowed clothes. "I feel as though I were Delia McGonigle," she said with a laugh.

Brian slid his glance from the road to Miranda. "Her clothes don't look even remotely the same on you. You're uniquely yourself, Miranda. No one even comes close."

"Delia told me they're the clothes she was engaged in."

"I can top that," Brian said roguishly.

Miranda pointedly stared out the window, but more to hide a smile than to conceal outrage. It was still early and a light drizzle dulled the tart green of the fields. "It's a soft day," Maureen had said at the door, looking out at the rain, so gentle as to be almost indistinguishable from mist. Miranda rolled down the car window and breathed deeply of the cool, rainy, earthy smell.

"You like it, don't you?" Brian said quietly, factually.

Miranda laughed. "I truly believe I'm half duck. Everyone else complains about the dampness and rain, while I take to it like—well—like a duck to water."

"You've come to the right place, then," Brian responded with a chuckle. "Thanks to its mild weather, even in winter, Killarney is known as the garden spot of Ireland; but what Killarney is really all about is water— the still water of the lakes, water flowing swift and clear in the rivers, drifting in mists, cascading down the mountainside, pouring out of the skies. Water is the source of Killarney's beauty, of her fickle light and color, her inconstant, changeable moods." He finished with a laugh and a sidelong glance at Miranda. "There, now I've gone poetic on you and you'll never forgive me." He put his hand out to her then and added quickly, "Ah, but let's not argue. It's a glorious morning in its own queer way and a beautiful time for you to see Innisfallen."

"Brian, no! This is not the time for sightseeing. I have a job to go to. I spent half the night playing Bogwoman, the other half sleeping—more or less—on a cold dirt floor. I'm in no shape for Innisfallen."

His eyes briefly touched the soft curve of her breasts under the thick, clinging sweater. His nostrils flared with amusement, and a wicked smile tilted the corners of his mouth upward. "I'd say you were in fine shape for Innisfallen—but not for a laboratory."

"And why not for a *laboratory,* Mr. O'Bannon?" Accenting the second syllable, she mimicked his pronunciation of the word.

"It would be a difficult transition, *macushla*. Look at that."

He stopped the car, and Miranda looked out at Lough Leane, the Lower Lake. Its glassy surface reflected the gray-bellied clouds massed low in the sky. Mist spilled like a silver waterfall over the islands in its center and draped the bulky shoulders of the mountains beyond. Everything was soft and muted, and Miranda understood what Brian meant about the difficulty of transition. The sterile whiteness of the laboratory, the harshness of the fluorescent lights, the constant hum of the centrifuges in the halls outside—all were as different from this as . . . as . . . science from poetry. She shot Brian a suspicious glance. Was he asking her to choose? But that was foolish. All that was involved was an hour's trip to a charming little island. She didn't punch a time-clock; she could report late for work once in a while. And hadn't she always promised herself she'd see Innisfallen sometime?

"How will we get out there?" she asked, not looking at him, so that she wouldn't have to see the triumph in his eyes.

"Fishermen often leave their boats in the sedge bordering the lake. We'll just borrow one."

Silently, they strode across a dew-soaked field and passed through a fringe of mist-silvered trees. They walked along the lake until they came upon an old wooden rowboat, its oars laid neatly in the bottom. As they shoved off from shore, a fly-over of crows chevroned its way across the sky—black against gray, their *caw, caw, caw* the only sound except for the soft lapping of the water against the oars.

Awed by the silence, the vastness of the lake, and the majesty of the mist-shrouded blue mountains, Miranda said, "It looks the way it must have at the beginning of time."

Brian nodded. "It does, particularly as the great lakes of Killarney are actually inland seas, formed in the ice age."

He looked off into the distance and Miranda studied his face, finding details she hadn't seen before—a horizontal crease in his broad, tanned forehead, a brown mole on his right temple, a small scar that ran into the cleft in his chin. His gaze returned to her, and she looked away so he wouldn't guess.

It had happened. Without thought or analysis, the knowledge had come to her in a lightning flash of revelation. She loved Brian. Whatever had held her back from loving him before might still exist, but it no longer mattered. Love wasn't anything to pussyfoot around with; it called for a flying leap. And she, Miranda Dunn, was hurtling through the air at that very moment.

Did Brian suspect?—perhaps. How else to explain that quizzical look he gave her as he tied up at the island's landing stage and helped her out of the boat?

"Welcome to the fairy isle of Innisfallen," he said.

"Fairy?"

"That's what Thomas Moore, the Irish poet, called it. There's a legend about the great O'Donoghue, the ancient chieftain of this region. Once every seven years, before the morning sun has cleared away the mists, the O'Donoghue comes riding over the lake on a snow-white horse, with fairies strewing flowers before him. As he approaches his ancient home, everything returns to its former state of grandeur—his castle, stables, and gardens. He rides into the mountains, where his treasure is. Then, just before the sun comes up, the O'Donoghue recrosses the water and vanishes, leaving behind the ruins of his castle again."

"What a charming story!"

"Charming, nothing! The O'Donoghue was a fighter. Let me do 'O'Donoghue's Call' for you." Brian jumped onto a rock and struck a dramatic pose, his strong chin jutting out and one arm extended.

> "Sound the Eagle's Whistle,
> Kerry's call to battle,
> Let the Eagle's Nest
> With its echoes rattle!"

He stopped and looked down at her. "Did I hear you ask for more?"

Red-faced with laughter, Miranda replied, "No, you didn't."

"Ah, well," Brian said, leaping off the rock, "it's probably modern poetry that seizes your heart."

Miranda pointed upward to a low cliff where a stone ruin with the rounded arch of a Romanesque doorway stood. "What's that building?"

"It's the remains of the famous monastery of Innisfallen, founded by Saint Finian the Leper in the seventh century. It was a center of learning when it wasn't being plundered by the Vikings or the Irish themselves. You might have heard of the *Annals of Innisfallen*."

Miranda looked blank and shook her head, so Brian continued, "They were written by the monks of this abbey in about 1215 and are an important source for the early history of Ireland." He put his arm around her waist then. "Come, let me show you the rest of the island."

As they walked along, Miranda exclaimed at the lushness of the vegetation. "That's *Ilex aquifolium*—holly," she said, pointing to an evergreen shrub with pointed, glossy leaves, "and *Epigaea repens,* trailing arbutus, or mayflower," she continued, looking at a vinelike plant on the ground, "and that's rowan," she added, indicating a small tree with clusters of bright red berries— "*Sorbus aucuparia.*"

His hold on her waist tightened, stopping her from taking another step. Turning her so she faced him and resting his hands on the swell of her hips, he looked into her eyes. "What are you trying not to tell me, *macushla?*"

Now's the time for that flying leap, Miranda told herself. But she found she couldn't even get off the ground. How could she come right out and say flatly, "I love you, Brian"? So she murmured, "I have no idea what you mean," and botched the whole effect with a haughty look that didn't come off under his quizzical gaze and with a schoolgirl blush that was a dead give-away.

He studied her for a moment, his expression a mixture of awe and tenderness and surprise. "So you've finally come round. The way you've been shilly-shallying, I thought we'd be octogenarians and unable..."

She put her finger on his lips and said in her own version of a Kerry brogue, "Sure and it's too bad it's a poet I have to love. They're all talk and no..."

An amused gleam turned his eyes an even more dazzling blue. He seized her hand and complained, "Is it making fun of both me language and me prowess you are, woman?" He took her finger in his mouth, biting it and licking it and sucking it, as all the time he watched her with that devilish glint in his eyes.

Oh my God, Miranda thought, if he can send all these little chills through me just fooling around with my finger, what will happen next? Aware of his intent, she turned her head as though this would alleviate the rapid beating of her heart. But when his large hands pulled her toward him and his arms held her close with all the strength of his need, a deep sigh escaped her. Her single and only wish—to love and be loved by Brian—was coming true, here on the fairy isle of Innisfallen.

His hard, well-muscled chest crushed her breasts as though they were fragile blossoms, and in the fit of their bodies she could feel the tautness in his thighs and the growing imperiousness of his desire. Yet his kiss began as a tender gift, demanding nothing from her but the softness of her lips and the smooth velvet of her mouth's interior. She moved a little, not from reluctance but from a sudden impulse to experience his lean, masculine body in another way.

With possessive urging, he flattened his palms against her back and brought her closer again. As if he were playing out some age-old atavistic drama of pursuit and capture, his kiss became rougher. His mouth rode hers hard, twisting and pressing against it, devouring it with moist, savage kisses, forcing her lips apart.

Breathing quickly, her blood charging through her veins, Miranda met his fierceness with her own matching hunger. She drew his tongue into the intimacy of her mouth, caressing it with her velvety tongue at the same time that she moved seductively against him.

The leader in their dance of love, Brian changed the tempo then. Tenderly, he lay his stubble-roughened cheek against her smooth face. "You're soft as a daisy petal and sweet as the white root of the green-growing grass." His lips wandered to her ear and he traced its shell-like convolutions, making her feel trembly and vulnerable with delight. "And I love you completely as everything in nature is complete and whole and perfect."

"And I love you, Brian, as . . ." She hesitated. She wasn't used to thinking in similes, and the terms that did come to mind were all biological. "Would it sound silly if I said 'with every cell in my body'? Because it's true, you know; that's how I feel."

Brian chuckled. "Why don't you leave the poetry but not"—his voice grew husky—"the loving to me."

His mouth swooped down to hers again in a kiss she wished would never end. There wasn't a part of him she didn't love, didn't want. Miranda slipped her hand inside his tweed jacket and up under his sweater. She passed her fingers over the smooth surface of his back and thought it the most wonderful skin in the world.

He nibbled at her lips and murmured against them, "Your hands are doing dangerous things to me, *ma-cushla*. Aren't you afraid?"

"Yes," she breathed. "And I love it."

His eyes narrow and hot with desire, he lifted her heavy sweater and the one underneath. Moving one hand restlessly across her back, he curved the other around her firm derriere and cupped her in even closer to him. Miranda thrilled to the pressure of his hardness against her, a harbinger of the joy to come.

She stretched upward to bite his ear and, braless under the two sweaters, raised her full breasts. Brian's hands reached for their ripeness. At his fondling of her soft flesh, Miranda moaned softly, aroused even further by the exquisite pleasure he was giving her.

"It's raining, love," he cautioned regretfully. "Are you sure you want to?"

"I'm half duck, remember?" Miranda whispered back. The dry turf of an oak-shaded glade received their clasped forms now. The heavy overhang of the trees around them was a closing of curtains. The utter quiet—the only sound the gentle dripping of the trees in the half mist, half drizzle—and the mysterious, silent lake and brooding mountains, and most of all the joy of love made Miranda feel as if she were indeed in an enchanted place. "Innisfallen really is a fairy isle," she murmured.

"With two very mortal lovers, I'm afraid," Brian said ruefully. "Will you be cold?"

Miranda stretched languorously and held up her arms for him. "I've got hot blood. It melts test tubes."

"Someday I'd like to make love to you in a proper bedroom instead of laboratory floors and muddy fields and bogs and Irish rain forests."

"Not *too* proper, I hope." She smiled wickedly up at him. "Do poets *always* talk this much before they make love? Did Shelley? Did Tennyson? Did—?" His mouth silenced her with a fiercely passionate kiss. When he finally released her, she said, pouting, "I was only trying to show how much I know."

His voice husky again as he looked at her, he replied, "I only want to know that you love me."

"There we go again—words, words, words." Miranda sat up and started to pull her Aran sweater up over her head. Her voice muffled by the heavy wool, she said, "Scientists believe in deeds."

"I insist on me answer," he said with mock stubbornness in a thick Irish brogue. He pulled the sweater off her, announcing triumphantly, "She loves me!" Then, with infinite, tantalizing slowness punctuated by several playfully exciting pauses on the way, he got the underlying green knit off and wailed, "She loves me not." He laid both sweaters on the ground for her, and Miranda relaxed into their softness. She stretched her arms out to him and held him close as his lips discovered the firm curves of her breasts, then nudged her sleepy nipples into delighted peaks. "Do you love me?" he asked again.

With a long, exultant laugh that sent a bird into a surprised morning song, Miranda said, "No answers are given on the fairy isle of Innisfallen. You'll have to find out for yourself."

"And that I will," he answered grimly. He unzipped the green corduroy skirt and, slipping his hands inside, eased it down Miranda's hips and off her. "She loves me!" he boasted, and Miranda laughed again. He took his jacket off then and carefully placed it over her.

"You've got to make it come out right," Miranda said, looking impishly up at him, "and only my panties are left."

"Leave it to me," he said confidently.

Sitting up, she tugged at his turtleneck jersey. "Two can play at this game."

But he caught her hands and forced her gently back onto the sweaters. "You don't have to. You already know

I love you and adore you and want you." Between feverish, desire-fueling kisses that covered her face and throat and shoulders, Brian divested himself of his clothes. He settled himself above her and slid his hands up under the silk of her bikini triangle, taking a long time to draw it over the peach-colored down of her thighs and legs.

"She loves me—not?" he questioned.

"I love you, Brian," Miranda breathed.

"And I will never love you more than I love you at this moment, *macushla*." He bent his head to her again, and rhythmically she ran her hands through his dark, tousled hair as he kissed the taut underside of each breast. Then, when he took each tight little nipple into his mouth, lightly, erotically grazing it with his teeth, her hands clenched at his shock of hair to ease the sweet, piercing ecstasy.

He loved her all over then with his lips and his bearded cheek and his long, sensitive fingers until she could feel a hot, moist unfurling in her loins. Knowing it would soon be satisfied, she played with the feeling, making its assuagement wait while she sampled other pleasures—the feel of his bare, muscled back under her hands, the wiry rasp of his chest hair against her soft breasts, the slow journey of his fingers up the inside of her thighs.

Suddenly, with lightning swiftness, there could be no more waiting for either of them. With the great cloudy sky above and the green earth beneath them, godlike, he drove into her waiting depths. Everything that was primitive and wild and elemental in Miranda broke forth. The earth itself seemed to move beneath her as her back arched and her hips surged up to meet Brian's. No inarticulate small moans and cries sufficed to express her rapture. An exultant paean of joy, a crescendo of ecstatic *O*'s, rang out through the trees. Her arms and legs tightened around him and her fingers curved and dug into the firm flesh of his buttocks. She was earthbound, and he, her powerful-loined Zeus, was setting her free, taking her with him up and up until a final driving thrust sent them over the crest—out into a starry firmament of whirling, fiery planets.

Then she was earth-tied again, and her splendid god, too—shot down out of the sky to lie intimately warm and heavy on top of her, his head cradled between her swollen breasts, his length pressed to hers under the tweed jacket. Inert as a rock, feeling herself part of the earth itself, Miranda lay still, beyond thought or even feeling. What was lacking in her had been completed; what was missing, filled in. Happiness had become the very stuff of her being; it was now her natural state.

She pressed her fingers lightly on Brian's bare back, just for the joy of feeling him. "Am I too heavy, *macushla?*" he asked.

Miranda laughed and teasingly moved one breast so it brushed against his lips. "Make your body light as a dancer's, as sure as a Mohawk brave's."

He reached around and pinched her lightly on the buttocks. "I'd say I was as sure as any Mohawk"—his pinch turned into a lingering caress—"or Iroquois"—his long, supple fingers were stroking her thighs now, arousing her desire again—"or . . ."

She brushed his hand away. "Ssh," she hissed. "I hear someone."

They dressed quickly and walked back to the landing stage. A pair of middle-aged, tweedy Britishers were establishing themselves on the shore—the man with a fishing pole and his wife with an easel and painting stool.

Polite nods were exchanged; then each couple restored the other to their original privacy.

"It's stopped raining," Miranda said, awestruck by

the fact that they hadn't noticed. "There's even a rainbow. Look!" She pointed to the multicolored arc shimmering in the watery sky.

"That's one thing to be said for making love in the great outdoors—you don't get sights like that in a bedroom." Brian's sapphire-blue eyes sparkled with laughter as he put his hand out to help her into the rowboat. "But who cares for scenery at a time like this? Your place, *macushla?*"

The postman always came early in Killarney, and Miranda found several letters on the carpet under the mail slot when she and Brian opened the door. One was a long, slim envelope, with Wolcott Research Institute printed on it. Miranda held it in her hand for a moment and stood looking at it.

"Something important?" Brian asked lightly.

"Not really. It can wait." She went to him then and, reaching up, ran her cool fingers down his cheek. "You need a shave. I have a razor."

He caught her hand and laid a kiss in the center of the palm. "Later, *macushla*. Unless my beard bothers you."

Miranda lay her smooth cheek against his now quite-sharp beard. "I love it," she whispered.

"And me? Do you love me?"

"I don't know," Miranda said thoughtfully. "I think perhaps it's irrelevant now. You're so much a part of me—of my nerves and bone and flesh—that you could have been formed from one of my own ribs. Is that love? I no longer know."

"It's love, *macushla,*" Brian said with quiet authority. "You can believe me."

"No blarney?" she asked mischievously.

"Not a word of it, but you're much too beautiful a

woman to be perpetually dressed in Irish wool. Don't
you have something else to put on?"

As he spoke, his hands moved enticingly down Miranda's breasts and over her hips. A current of longing
ran through her, and her breath quickened. "I think I
have something that's not wool," she said demurely.

"Good! Even sackcloth would be a welcome change."

Miranda left him and went to her bedroom. She took
a fuchsia-colored satin nightgown, trimmed with lace,
from her drawer and slipped it over her head. It fell in
shimmering ripples of color to the floor. Her breasts
pushed the patterned lace into softly mounding blossoms,
and the satin clung to her firm belly and rounded hips.
She brushed her hair until it shone like sheets of beaten
gold. Then she anointed herself with a sensuous floral
perfume and went to him.

Brian had moved into the living room and was looking
through a book when she entered. He got to his feet and
whispered, "Miranda *acree,* how beautiful you are."

"Sheila is my Irish dictionary, but she's at Biochem.
What does *acree* mean, Brian?"

"It means 'my love,' and that's what you are." He
took her hand then, and she led him into her bedroom.
Hungry as they still were for each other, they turned day
into night and celebrated their love while it rained and
cleared up and rained again in Killarney.

"We're probably missing lots of rainbows," Miranda
said as she awakened from a light sleep and glanced out
the window.

Brian grunted, stretched luxuriously, and folded his
arms around her again. "You don't know how great it is
to be in a bed with you instead of..."

Miranda laughed, executed a little wiggle to bring her
now-bare body closer to his, and interrupted, "...a muddy

field, a bog, and an Irish rain forest—I know."

"I have to go up to Dublin on business soon. We could repeat this delightful experience, there being no bogs, fields, or forests in Dublin that I know of. What do you say, *macushla?*"

"I say yes—if I can get the time off, and I'm reasonably sure that I can, inasmuch as I've finished the experiments I was working on and have a vacation coming to me."

"I'm sure Walter would let you go."

She raised herself on one elbow and looked down at him. With bland innocence, she said, "If not, I suppose you could always bribe him with another salmon." Then she got moody. "Ph.D.'s come cheap these days."

Brian's azure blue eyes sparkled with glee. He comforted her with his hands, then pulled her down on top of him. As he helped her accommodate her body over his, he whispered devilishly, "Sure it wasn't a salmon at all; it was the biggest brown trout in all Ireland."

Brian's smile fueled the blaze in Miranda's heart, and with his hands slowly stroking her smooth flesh in long, thrilling sweeps from her shoulders to her thighs, she said, "Give him anything he asks for, darling, just so long as we can go to Dublin together."

Later, after Brian had left, Miranda went to her little stack of mail. She felt cloud-borne with happiness and free-floating as a kite: only one string tied her to earth—her love for Brian. She opened the envelope from Wolcott gingerly, using just the tips of her fingers. The only good news it could contain now was that she hadn't gotten the fellowship, but life didn't work that way. Miranda read on quickly until she found what she was seeking—she had a month before she would have to report to the institute. She slowly refolded the letter.

I won't tell Brian, she thought. I won't even think about a decision until after we return from Dublin. Miranda tapped the letter against her thumbnail. Even if she didn't accept the fellowship, that wouldn't mean she was forsaking her work for Brian. Or would it? Her father would certainly think so. He'd be furious if she rejected this opportunity.

For a moment, a familiar little-girl fear of disappointing her father caused a catch in Miranda's steady heartbeat. Then she put the letter back in its envelope and pensively tucked it away in her desk. With rueful irony, she remembered that unlike most children, she had often longed for a parent who cared not more, but less about her.

Chapter Eight

THE FIRST THING the following morning, Miranda went to Walter Royce's office. She paused by Sheila's desk and watched for a moment as the secretary whited out a word on a sheet of bond in her typewriter.

A dictionary and a bottle of liquid eraser lay at Sheila's elbow, and she looked up at Miranda with a wry expression on her pert face. "It's a whole jug of that stuff I need, not a wee bottle like that. And if you want to see himself, it's my advice that you not bother. He's in bad humor today."

"I shall beard the lion in his den," Miranda said gaily. "Unless he's busy."

Sheila shook her head. "Just knock and listen for the roar."

At the growled "Come in," Miranda rolled her eyes comically and opened the door.

"You look mighty chipper this morning," Walter said sourly, raising his head from a mass of papers on his desk.

"That's because I'm going on vacation—I hope."

Her chief waved a magnanimous hand. "If you're all caught up, go ahead. I know you have time coming to you. I only wish to hell I could," he continued bitterly, looking down at his desk. "Administration! I hate it. I became a scientist so I could work in a lab, not push paper around."

"Would two weeks be all right?"

"If that's what's coming to you, take it." He fixed her with his shrewd eyes. "Where are you going? It's none of my business"—he grinned momentarily—"but Janet will want to know."

Miranda steadfastly returned his gaze. "To Dublin— with Brian." Her heart beat a little faster as she waited for his response to her candor. Although she felt no shame in going away with the man she loved, it was sometimes hard to tell what the reaction of the older generation would be to this situation.

Somewhat to Miranda's relief, Walter's gloomy expression gave way to a delighted smile. "Good for you, Miranda," he said heartily. "Brian's a great guy and . . . well, you've got some . . . romance coming to you." His pale blue eyes twinkled then behind his rimless glasses. "I won't tell Frazier."

Miranda stared at him in surprise. She was a grown woman. What business of her father's could it possibly be if she went away with her lover?

On her way past Sheila's desk again, Miranda looked over the young woman's shoulder. She pointed to a word Sheila had already typed. "That should be an *i*, Sheila."

"Oh, no, not another one. The wastebasket's full of me mistakes." She whispered conspiratorially to Miranda, "I fill my purse with them as the day goes on and take them home, so himself won't see how full the basket is."

Miranda smiled and said, "I'm going on vacation for two weeks, Sheila."

"I'll keep your paycheck and mail for you, miss, although I doubt that you'll be thinking much of the office while you're away." Sheila's words were innocent enough, but the look on her face made Miranda flush a little. She wasn't used to having *everybody* know her business; was love a flag that one carried unfurled? Then she smiled back at Sheila. Who better than another woman could know how she felt?

It was almost embarrassing to be so happy, to have all the old clichés—walking on air, head in the clouds— come into one's mind. Miranda looked out her bedroom window and laughed as she added "and singing in the rain." She slammed the lid down on her suitcase. She was all packed and ready for Brian to pick her up. They were taking the train up to Dublin, where they would stay in a town house owned by a wealthy friend of Brian's.

"We need a taste of city life for a change," Brian had said. "Besides, there's that poetry reading I'm scheduled for, and I want to see my literary agent about a book I have in mind. It's a subject that would interest you, I think, since it would be based loosely on the lectures on poetry and science that I gave at Biochem."

Miranda's gaze returned to her suitcase. While Brian was busy with his meetings, she would go shopping in Dublin's famous Grafton Street. She would buy soft, clinging dresses and nightgowns of the most alluring style and material she could find. She was going to have a honeymoon—her first *real* one.

Miranda and Brian had a first-class carriage to themselves on the three-and-a-half-hour train trip to Dublin. They sat side by side, reveling in the coziness and privacy of the little compartment. As the green of the countryside and the assorted pastel colors of the houses in the little towns sped by their rain-streaked window, Brian told her about his family and the pull he had once felt between their simple values, rooted in the soil and the simplicity of tradition, and his own constantly evolving complex view of life.

"From the beginning, I was different," he said, "because I read books and tried to write—stories mostly, and some poetry. Yet I always pulled my weight on the farm," he added a little defensively. "But when I was young, there was this feeling of disloyalty, too, as though by not being like my family, I was somehow denying them."

"And how did you resolve this problem?" Miranda asked softly.

"It was a woman who helped me indirectly, and I want to tell you about her so you'll know all there is to know about me."

A woman? Was this someone he had loved more than he loved her? Miranda's hand went loose and slack in his, as though suddenly she had no right to this little sign of affection.

"It all happened when I went up to Trinity. I was pretty raw—a real country boy. I went to a poetry reading one night in town and met a young woman who came from an aristocratic 'county' family. We fell in love and planned to marry, whereupon I knocked myself silly trying to be the kind of man she and her parents wanted. I switched for a time to the study of law, a more respectable profession than poetry, went fox-hunting at their country home, and all in all made a bloody fool of myself. I didn't realize how much of a fool until my parents and older brother came up to Dublin to visit me one weekend. At first I thought their surprise—and disgust—at my behavior was due to jealousy. Then I saw that it was the loss of my true self—the farm lad turned poet—that they deplored. In understanding that, I realized that they accepted me better than I accepted myself. They didn't construe my not following their ways as disloyalty. On the contrary, whereas perhaps before there had been a little jealousy, there was none now. Indeed, they were proud of me because I was a scholar— but not yet, I'm afraid, a gentleman."

"Did this woman love you?"

"She loved the idea of me," Brian said with a grin. "As a somewhat unconventional young poet, I was part of her rebellion against her family and society. But when marriage was in the offing, it turned out that she wanted me to conform to the mores of her class, after all. Eventually, I came to my senses, and so did she, I suppose, since she married a neighboring landowner. Presumably, they've been happy ever since, chasing foxes together."

"And was this the only woman you ever loved?" It's stupid to be jealous, but I have to know, Miranda thought.

Brian threw his head back and laughed. "God love you, no, *macushla,* but she was the only one I loved seriously enough to have it change me—until I met you."

"That love made you pretty silly, by your own admission. How will ours change you, do you think?" Miranda studied him.

Brian took a strand of her hair and rubbed it between two fingers. "Your hair is the pale gold of ripe barley," he mused. He let it fall and continued gravely, "I don't know yet how our love will change me, but I know it won't be in the same way. After all, what's the good of making mistakes if you don't use them?"

What indeed? Miranda wondered, thinking of Craig. But suppose you didn't know the mistake you had made? Then how could you avoid repeating it?

They took a cab from Dublin's Heuston Station to their borrowed town house, going down broad O'Connell Street and past the columned façade of the General Post

Office, where the Easter Rising of 1916 began. They crossed O'Connell Bridge, the main span over the steel-gray Liffey, and rode by the many exquisite examples of Georgian architecture, which Dublin, more than any other of the world's great cities, still retained from the eighteenth century.

As the cab turned into Merrion Square, Miranda delighted in the sight before her. She had been in Dublin many times, but the classical beauty of its buildings always pleased her anew. She was looking now at a row of wren-brown brick town houses that formed a square around a lush green park. The uniformity of the dun-colored brick and the perfect proportions of the regularly spaced windows created an effect of dignity and repose that Miranda appreciated.

The symmetry of the houses was relieved by the doors. Each was topped by a semicircular spider's-web fanlight and flanked by classical pillars painted cream, while the delicately paneled doors themselves were vivid greens and blues and orangy reds, the colors punctuated by polished brass knockers.

"The square is beautiful, isn't it?" Brian said. "My friend's house was built in 1755. He rescued it from a firm of solicitors who were totally insensitive to its architecture." He opened the front door and looked down at her lovingly. "I won't carry you across *this* threshold. There's another I infinitely prefer."

Still outside, Miranda glanced behind her at the rows of lace-curtained windows. "You're frustrating a lot of people."

He brushed his lips lingeringly over her hair and whispered, "Just so long as it isn't a certain poet and biologist."

Inside, a matching fanlight capped the hall doorway, beyond which hung a Waterford crystal chandelier and the steps of a gracefully curving staircase bordered by

walls in Wedgwood blue and white. A demure, black-
frocked maid named Anna showed Miranda to her room
on the third floor, overlooking the park.

"I thought you would prefer your own room," Brian
said, entering as soon as the maid had left. "I have the
'connecting,' with a bath between." He pointed his square
chin toward a door set in the east wall.

"We share a bath?"

"Bath, bed, and breakfast." He took her in his arms
and nibbled deliciously at her lips.

"What does the maid think?" Miranda asked, a worried little frown appearing on her smooth forehead.

"That we're rich and married and practicing birth control," Brian said with an unmistakable smirk. He glanced
at his watch. "She's prepared a cold supper for us, and
unless you've something more for her to do, she'll leave
for the day."

Miranda laughed. "I've already had more done for me
than I'm used to. Anna's unpacked my bag, hung up my
clothes, built a fire in that exquisite Georgian fireplace,
and drawn a bath, which I'm going to use right now. So
far as I'm concerned, you may dismiss her."

"Right! I'll also lay out the cold vittles." He ran his
eyes down the flame-colored wool dress she wore. "Don't
feel you have to dress for dinner—at all," he said seductively.

And surprising herself, Miranda, who never ate in a
nightgown or bathrobe, took him at his word. The warm,
scented bath in the old-fashioned, claw-footed tub so
relaxed her that she didn't feel like getting dressed again.
So she wrapped herself in a hooded terry-cloth Wedg-
wood-blue guest robe that she found hanging on a hook
on the bathroom door and padded downstairs to Brian.

She found him in the modernized kitchen, setting out
platters of cold meats and cheeses and fruits.

He looked up as she came in and made a silent *O*

with his lips. "I think you're going to have a speechless poet on your hands, Miranda. You're really too lovely for words." He put down the dish he was holding and went to her. Pulling her close to him with one hand, he pushed the bathrobe hood back off her hair with the other. "You looked a bit like a nun in blue habit the other way," he explained.

"My hair's still damp from my bath."

"I'll dry it for you in front of your fire." He scooped her up in his arms and carried her up the elegant staircase to her bedroom. "This is the threshold I wanted to carry you across." He bent his head and kissed the tiny, throbbing pulse at the side of her neck. Then he nudged the robe open with his lips, letting them go lower and lower until the creamy slope of her breast appeared. He traced its soft curves with moist, open-mouthed kisses that made her blood flow hot and fast like the licking flames of a fire.

Advancing into the room, Brian picked up a brush and a hand mirror from the bureau and, after a detour to the bathroom for a thick delft-blue towel, seated himself in a wing armchair in front of the fire with Miranda on his lap. He rubbed her hair with the towel briskly, almost roughly, until it stuck out stiffly from her head.

Miranda looked in the hand mirror Brian had given her to hold, and laughed. "I look like a blond porcupine."

"Please wait, *madame,*" Brian said in a heavy French accent. "Monsieur Henri, the famous hairdresser from Paris, will put all to rights again."

Brian sat her up straight on his lap and closed the bathrobe around her. "Please, *madame,* even a French *artiste* cannot concentrate on his work under such conditions of temptation."

"The guy who dressed the hair of Venus de Milo didn't have any trouble with temptation."

"Judging from the satisfied look on that lady's face,

I wouldn't be too sure." Brian drew the brush through Miranda's amber locks in long, smooth sweeps over and over again until, lulled almost to sleep by the repetitive motions and the warmth of the fire, Miranda lay back in Brian's arms, letting the robe fall open, and closed her eyes. Brian kissed her eyelids and moved his hand enticingly inside the robe.

She brushed his hand aside and sat up straight. "My hairdressers don't usually..." she began with mock haughtiness.

"But Henri is not just an ordinary *coiffeur*. Look, *madame!*" Brian steadied the mirror for her and Miranda looked into it, laughing. Surveying the smooth pageboy he had created, she said, "It's terrific. If the bottom ever falls out of poetry..."

His hand slid down and curved around her buttocks; at the same time he laid his face along the smooth flesh of her throat. "I'll be so drunk with the joy of you, I won't even notice, *macushla*."

The slow sliding of his hand up and down her thigh was producing a luscious expanding warmth throughout Miranda's body. She was fast approaching a state of spontaneous explosion. Reaching for his hand, she stayed it and, looking piteously up into his face, said, "I'm hungry, Brian."

"I know, love," he said dreamily, renewing his sensuous stroking of her legs. "But you won't be much longer."

"I mean for *food!* I'm famished, starved, ravenous!"

"I'll feed you, *macushla*." He gave an exaggerated sigh of resignation. "You'll never have the dimensions of a Venus de Milo if I don't. How does supper in bed strike you?"

"*Supper* in bed?"

"Much better than breakfast, with the sheets all crunchy from toast crumbs and yellow with egg yolk."

With that, he lifted her in his arms and took the few steps to the bed. Tossing back the coverlet, he placed her between the cool sheets and put an extra pillow behind her head.

"Where are *you* going to eat?" Miranda asked, still in a slight state of wonder about his plans.

"Oh, I'm going to join you." The expression on his face was blandly innocent, but his clear blue eyes gleamed with laughter.

A short while later, he appeared with a tray holding two turkey sandwiches cut in quarters, fruit, cubes of cheese, and a bottle of white wine and two polished cut-crystal glasses. He placed the tray on the nightstand and said, "Start, if you like. I'll be with you in a jiffy."

She took several bites of a turkey sandwich and watched as he undressed. Finally, powerful and shaggy-chested, he eased himself into bed and reached across her for the wine. He poured each of them a glass.

"What will we drink to?" Miranda asked.

"How about drinking to an old Irish saying I just made up?"

"Which is?" she said warily.

"That love must lie down in laughter or indifference will soon be its bedfellow."

Puzzled by what he might have in mind, she could only look at the crisp, upturned corners of his mouth and his laughing blue eyes. He tweaked her robe and said with mock gravity, "This will have to come off."

Her bewilderment deepening, Miranda asked, "Is this a ritual?"

"It could be called that," he answered absently, his eyes still serious and focused on her robe. Miranda shrugged herself out of the garment and let it fall over the side of the bed. Reaching across her again, Brian took the bowl of fruit from the tray and looked down at her, his expression deeply thoughtful.

"Here, I think, and here," he said, draping a small cluster of grapes around each pink pearl at the tip of her breast.

"Brian! What are you doing?" Miranda almost screamed.

"Turning you into a harvest goddess," he answered calmly. "It's an old Irish custom."

"Baloney!" she said explosively.

"No, love, I don't think so. Too high in cholesterol. I didn't tell you, but I have to watch that."

"What *are* you going to do?" Miranda asked sharply.

But Brian ignored her question. Looking down at her as though she were an unclothed, inanimate mannequin and he a window-dresser, he said, "I think maybe a cherry right here." With that, he put a cherry in her navel with the stem sticking out. "And . . ." Musing, he let his gaze drift down her body.

"Brian!" But the soft scream turned into a delighted giggle as, murmuring, "One of the rules is no hands," he tried to pluck a cluster of grapes off her nipple, failed, then chased it with his warm, moist mouth across her breast, down her belly, and to the place where he finally caught it. He continued to deck her with fruit and, with more or less dexterity, to remove it from her body. Finally, red-faced and out of breath and laughing, he lay back against the pillow and said, "Now that you know how to play the game, it's your turn."

His licking and kissing, nibbling and mouthing in so many sensitive places had aroused Miranda unbearably. Only her wish to win in this game of love motivated her to quell her desire for him, at least temporarily. So she "worshiped" him, as he had her, calling him her harvest god and decking him out with fruits and even the cubes of cheese, then taking them away in quick, tantalizing, grabbing kisses.

Brian's control went first. His laughing eyes intense

and hot now, he took her in his arms and made fervent, hurried love to her. When Miranda sighed with disappointment afterward, he whispered against her hair, "Love is a moveable feast, *macushla*." Before she knew what he was about, he had thrown the down-filled duvet that covered the bed onto the floor and placed her gently on it. He made love to her then with infinite slowness, using ways that only an experienced, sensitive man could know to bring her again and again to the peak of rapture.

Later, when she lay in his arms, sated and tired and infinitely happy, it occurred to her that sex would always be like this with Brian—adventurous and playful, open and trusting. In a further flash of insight, Miranda saw that Brian's creativity was whole, that his poetry derived in part from his sexual passion, and that his passion was creative, like his poetry.

Rousing herself, she bent over him where they both still lay curled up in the rumpled duvet on the floor, the purple grapes and hothouse cherries and russet pears scattered around them glowing jewellike in the light from the fire. "You know Innisfallen . . ." she began conversationally, giving the *s* the *sh* Irish sound.

"Do I ever!" Brian said emphatically, looking up at her with mischievous, laughing eyes.

Her own dark brown eyes answered the look in his. "Suppose one of the gentry of that fairy isle cast a spell to make me ask you a very dangerous question?"

"You're not one of those girl reporters posing as an eminent scientist, are you?" He creased his broad forehead in a frown.

"I'd do anything for a story," Miranda simpered.

"Anything?" Brian waggled his eyebrows a couple of times in a comical leer.

"Anyway, this perfectly dumb leprechaun—"

"Ssh, not so loud," Brian said, looking around the room.

"—is making me ask, if you had to choose between poetry and me, which would you choose?"

A broad grin spread across Brian's face. "Right now, poetry. But ask me again in about ten minutes, *macushla*."

He fell asleep so suddenly that Miranda could hardly believe it. That had been a silly question to ask him. She hadn't even meant it—she had just been fooling around. Still, if it came right down to it and he really had to, would he choose poetry over her? She looked down at Brian's handsome face, happy and relaxed in sleep, and shrugged, a wryly amused little smile on her face. Her question had been even sillier than she imagined. Men never had to make those choices. Brian could have her *and* his precious poetry.

Chapter Nine

OVER THE NEXT few days Brian showed Miranda parts of Dublin she hadn't yet seen. These included the places where some of Ireland's great writers—Sheridan and Swift, Wilde and Shaw, Yeats and O'Casey—had been born, lived, or died. In the spirit of their literary tour, they stopped for a few "jars," as the Irish put it, at an old-fashioned pub that had been a haunt of the poet Brendan Behan. Miranda ordered a Guinness, the famous stout from the two-hundred-year-old brewery near the Heuston Station. After a few swallows, the creamy foam that formed what was called a "Roman collar" on the rich, dark brown beer made a moustache over her upper lip. Not caring who saw him, even in this workingmen's beer parlor, Brian leaned forward and kissed the moustache away.

Another day, Brian took her to the house where Bram Stoker, the author of *Dracula,* had lived for a short time. While Miranda was reading the information on the circular blue plaque used to identify the houses of notables,

Brian said flippantly, "Parliament's just across the road. Not that I'm making any connection, mind you, between our high taxes and the proximity of the man who created the prototype of bloodsuckers." Finally, as the grande finale to their literary tour of Dublin, he took her to north Dublin and they retraced in part the historic walk of Leopold Bloom, the hero of James Joyce's *Ulysses*.

Although she had been there before, Miranda wanted to see Trinity College again, not only because it was Brian's alma mater, but because the austere beauty of its magnificent cobblestoned courtyard, velvet lawns and trees, and classically proportioned buildings pleased her deeply. It amazed her that simply by passing under an arched portico one could leave behind a noisy, congested street in the heart of the city and find oneself, as if in a time warp, in an academic cloister with the appearance and ambience of eighteenth-century Dublin.

Brian showed her the auditorium where his poetry reading would take place, then walked with her to the Long Room of Trinity's old library for another look at the Book of Kells. The long, narrow room with its high barrel-vaulted ceiling resembled the nave of a Gothic cathedral. On both sides of the aisle stood gleaming marble busts, and behind them rose tiers of ancient, leatherbound books whose soft brown richness merged with the darker wood of the paneled walls.

Miranda and Brian joined the line at the glass case containing the ninth-century illuminated manuscript that was called the Book of Kells because it reputedly came from the monastery of Kells in County Meath. Each page showed a scene from the life of Christ and the Evangelists, done in subtle colors produced by a yet-undiscovered ink. Around each scene was an intricately designed border, and every page commenced with an initial letter entwined with fantastic birds and animals, angels, and grotesque monsters.

Finally, hand in hand, they left Trinity College and walked back to Merrion Square, under a rapidly moving sky of gray and black clouds. The rain came before they reached the town house, and they burst through the door, laughing, their hair plastered to their wet faces and their shoes squishing water. They were met by the maid, Anna, who dimpled and smiled and practically curtsied as she told them she had laid a fire in madam's bedroom, was leaving a casserole in the fridge, and would be going now, if it was all right with them.

"She knows we're not married," Miranda whispered as, arms around each other's waist, they went upstairs in stockinged feet.

"Anna doesn't care. She's in love herself. His name's Sean, and he's an apprentice electrician. They're going to get married as soon as they can afford to. I promised to write a poem for their wedding, what's called an epithalamium."

Miranda was touched by the famous poet's promising to write a poem for the wedding of a domestic employee he hardly even knew. "You're a sweet man," she said as they entered her bedroom and Brian shut the door behind them.

"*Sweet* is it! And just when I was planning to rip your bodice—or at least your silk blouse—throw you on the bed, and ravish you."

Miranda cowered against the wall and crossed her arms over her chest. "You can ravish me all you want, but please don't rip my bodice. It cost fifty clams at a well-known New York department store, and I've worn it only once."

He threw his head back haughtily, turned on his heel, and strode away. "All right, I'll save the silk bodice but not what's underneath. Your virtue means nothing to me, my beauty." He whirled around suddenly, his eyes dancing, a wicked grin slashing white across his tanned face. "Unless . . . unless you yourself can hold onto your virtue whilst playing a certain game with me."

"What game, sire?" Miranda asked timidly.

Brian raised his eyebrows several times in a mock leer. "The game of illuminated manuscripts."

If I live to be a hundred and even if I never see him again, I will never forget this afternoon with the rain tearing at the windows and the fire inside and he and I in bed together, his wonderfully long, sensitive fingers and warm mouth tracing all over my body those magnificent, intricate capital letters, and demons and angels and mythical beasts, "illuminating" me to the point of a terrible, yearning need.

"Brian," Miranda breathed, as her supple body arched wildly in reaction to the soft, open-mouthed kiss he was drawing along the inside of her thigh, "your illuminated manuscript could light up Dublin. In fact, it's burning up. What letter are we on now?" she moaned. She tossed her head from side to side and dug her fingers into his smooth flesh. "Skip a few. Make it *z* now, will you, darling?" *What do Irish women call their men at moments like this? Ooh, I'm losing my mind . . . no, I'm not, only I don't think they did things like this in the Middle Ages . . . in Camelot . . . Camelot?*

"Brian!" Miranda's voice rose as his kiss reached the moist, throbbing center of her desire. "Now! Please!"

Just before he sealed their union and as he once more made love to her with his hands and mouth, he whispered, "There are hundreds of pages in those illuminated manuscripts and thousands of capitals, all of them different, and the love we'll make day after day will be just as wonderful and various as they are, *macushla.*"

Folded against him afterward, her face buried in the soft pelt on his chest, Miranda wished there were a magic spell she could call upon to hold her in that room with Brian forever, the rain slashing the windows and the fire keeping them cozy and warm.

The day of Brian's poetry reading, Miranda decided to buy a new dress—a dress to celebrate her happiness, to honor her lover, to please her man. Brian went with her to the shops on fashionable Grafton Street in the heart of Dublin, and Miranda took a special pleasure in modeling different possibilities for him and in his interested responses. And when he finally said, about a teal-blue silk dress with black stripes, "That looks smashing on you, Miranda," she swallowed hard at the soft, shining look in his eyes.

The dress required new shoes and a shorter slip than Miranda had, and there were a few other items she needed. As she went from store to store, Brian trotted beside her, carrying her packages and putting his hand under her elbow from time to time to steer her through the bustling, fast-paced lunch-hour crowd and the pavement artists, mimes, musicians, and flower sellers who occupied the pedestrian walkway of Grafton Street.

"You'd make a wonderful husband," Miranda said, with an amused sidelong glance at him.

"Isn't that what I've been after telling you, woman?"

Miranda laughed, as she always did when he jokingly assumed a heavy brogue. The light, spontaneous laugh was followed by a quiet glow that spread through her, warming, it seemed to Miranda, every cell in her body. Marriage had never been mentioned, but it had been tacitly understood that they would marry. All that remained was to make the actual plans. But suddenly doubt stabbed her like a traitor. Would marriage destroy their love? Would that grinning, rattling, unidentified skeleton she had shoved back into the closet so she could love Brian *let* her marry him?

"You're awfully quiet," Brian said. "I know that look; you need a Guinness, exhausted as you are from trying on every shoe in Dublin. Let's have lunch. I'm ready to drop, myself."

He took her to a place with mahogany paneling and crisp chrysanthemum-white tablecloths, where businessmen in dark suits ate Dublin Bay prawns and drank white wine or creamy-topped pints of Guinness. For the first course, Brian ordered Wexford mussels, breaded and cooked in garlic butter. They went on to saddle of lamb and little boiled potatoes, and finished with a hot apple tart and cream.

"It's a good thing I did all my shopping before lunch," she said as they left the restaurant. "I'm so full, I couldn't decide between two Irish linen handkerchiefs right now."

"It's between two Irish linen sheets that you should be, *macushla,* all plump and well nourished as you are."

"Brian!" she objected as, taking her arm, he hurried her out of Grafton Street to Dawson Street on the way to Merrion Square. "You have a poetry reading tonight."

"I'm well aware of that fact, love."

"Don't you have to prepare or practice—or something?"

He shook his head. "Every poem is engraved in my memory." He looked sidelong, lovingly, at her. "And on my heart."

As they approached the house in Merrion Square, they saw Anna closing the peacock-blue door behind her. "We've set the date, Mr. O'Bannon," she called out gaily. "Sean got a promotion. I've finished my work, and I'm off to meet him now."

"Congratulations, Anna," Brian replied. "I'll get busy on that poem right away."

"Aw, sure," the young woman said, blushing. "You've got plenty of time. The banns haven't even been said yet."

A short while later as they stood before the fire in her bedroom and Brian started to undress her, Miranda said archly, "Shouldn't you be working on Anna's nuptial poem?"

"I'm working on my own nuptial poem at the moment, *macushla.*" Slowly, he undid the cloth-covered buttons of her sheer, multicolor georgette blouse and lowered the straps of her lace-trimmed slip and then the straps of her bra. He lifted one soft, thrusting breast out of the wisp of silk containing it and kissed it all over tenderly. Then he took the pink rosette at the tip between his teeth and tugged gently at it, and a tropical flower unfurled deep inside Miranda, expanding, warm and trembling, throughout her body, lying open to his hands and mouth and body.

As he slipped the blouse off her shoulders, he murmured, "She loves me." He blanketed her smooth white flesh with kisses, then lifted her slip over her head, saying mischievously, "She loves me not."

Laughing now, Miranda joined in the game, undressing him slowly and kissing the place from which she removed each garment. It took a little cheating, but they managed to make it come out right.

"She loves me!" Brian said triumphantly as he eased her sheer panty hose down her thighs.

"He loves me!" Miranda answered, kneeling on the floor to remove an Argyl sock.

Brian's audience for his Dublin poetry reading was a far cry from the one at Biochem's Killarney plant. The large auditorium was filled literally to overflowing; people stood in the rear and students sat cross-legged on the stage. Several well-known Irish writers were there, and so were members of the press. There was even a television crew in position.

Miranda looked with amused pride at her lover as he

walked to the podium. This time he was the result of *her* handiwork. She had washed his hair and brushed it smooth. She had instructed the laundry to put enough starch in his shirt so that the collar wouldn't wilt midway through the evening. She had taken his tweed jacket out to be pressed and had helped him pick out a handsome, high-priced tie. Last, she had checked his shoes—both were brown, and his socks matched, too.

As his strong, resonant voice filled the auditorium, Miranda closed her eyes, the better to catch the subtle rhythms of his verse and visualize the images the poems called up. But an uneasy feeling at what she was hearing began to mount in her. Confused and disturbed, she opened her eyes. Brian's blissful expression and the emotional, sincere tones were a dead giveaway. The love poems he was reading were about her.

If she'd had any doubt, the poem that he called "Il-luminations" would have cinched her conviction. The poem didn't actually describe the game they had played, but the rain and the fire were there. Its theme was the nearly spiritual transcendence of self that the poet had experienced through his sexual union with a loved one. It was a beautiful poem and one that, judging from their breath-holding attentiveness, moved the audience. But as she listened, Miranda felt a rising indignation at the thought that he had used her as material for his poetry, that he had violated the tacit rules of privacy and intimacy not only by writing about their love but, worse, by read-ing the poem aloud to an auditorium full of strangers.

Not caring that he would see her leave, Miranda got up and, excusing herself softly to her neighbors, made her way to the end of the third row. As she marched up the aisle, she heard Brian's voice falter behind her. But head high, she maintained her relentless stride toward the door and, outside, continued walking rapidly until she reached Merrion Square.

Anna had been given the night off, but Miranda wasn't used to having a maid pack for her, anyway. She threw her clothes into her suitcase, made a reservation for a flight that night to London, and telephoned for a cab. Throughout, her lips were a tight, unyielding line.

It was her fault. How stupid did you have to be to get involved with a poet? Pretty stupid, evidently. By the very nature of his so-called profession, he was frivolous, immoral, even vicious; because it was vicious to cannibalize other people as provender for poetry. If she wanted to be generous, the most she could say was that he lacked the solidity of the men she worked shoulder-to-shoulder with in the lab. Miranda laughed shortly. And speaking of scientists, she could never imagine Frazier Dunn pulling a stunt like that. It was unthinkable!

When the doorbell rang and Miranda opened the door to the cabby, the full import of what she was doing struck her for the first time. She had been too angry before even to think. Now she realized that to leave without telling Brian the reason would be a violation of her principles. She glanced at her watch. The program should be over and all the congratulations said. Brian would be home soon. Miranda asked the driver to wait. She would be brief, and the break would be clean. Afterward, there would be nothing—no letters, no phone calls, and no messages sent through friends. While she waited, she checked the closets and bureaus. She wanted nothing of hers to remain.

She didn't hear him come in, only his voice taut with worry behind her as she bent over a drawer. "Why did you leave, *macushla?* Are you ill? I came as soon as I could."

Miranda straightened up and faced him. His worried look made her love for him tear through her with the crackling force of a lightning bolt. Then it was gone, tamped down by her angry memory of "Illuminations."

"I left because I didn't want to hear the most intimate experience a man and a woman can have put on exhibition for the greater glory of Brian O'Bannon."

"I'll ignore that last bit," Brian said grimly, "but notice that you said 'a man and a woman.' Therein lies your answer to why I wrote 'Illuminations'—I presume that's the poem you're objecting to—and why I read it."

"'Therein lies your answer,'" she mimicked sarcastically. "What's coming next—more of your blarney? Do you really expect me to stand here and listen to you try to get around me?"

"I expect you to listen to my explanation because you owe it to me," he said, biting off his words as he spoke. Eyes blazing, a shock of pitch-black hair spilling over his forehead, he advanced toward her and seized her by the shoulders.

The contact galvanized them both. Under his touch, she felt boneless and weak. If he had taken her in his arms then and laid his face gently against hers, she would have made up with him, she thought. But he was too angry or too proud for that; whether it was disappointment at his not doing so or her own righteous anger being refueled, Miranda didn't know, but her disillusionment with him increased.

"As I started to say before," he continued sternly, "it's just because love *is* the most intimate experience a man and a woman can have that I can write about it. It's a universal experience. Can't you see that?"

"I know love is a universal experience," she snapped. "That's a pretty simple concept. What I'm talking about is basing a poem on *our* intimate experience—yours and mine, Brian and Miranda, not a man and a woman." The words came pouring out of her like molten lava. Reliving the experience had made her even angrier than before. The fact that his lustrous, dark blue eyes had softened with compassion didn't change her feelings. Among other

things, he had wounded her pride, and pity was no balm
to hurt pride.

"If you stopped and thought about it for a while or if
I gave you a copy of the poem to read, I think you'd see
it wasn't that revealing," he said reasonably.

But she was not going to let her feelings be denied.
She knew what "Illuminations" was about, and even if
she and Brian were the only people in the world to understand the poem, she believed she would still be jus-
tified in objecting to it.

"It was more revealing than I can accept," she said
firmly. "I don't think we see things the same way, Brian.
We have different value systems. We're two parallel train
tracks going nowhere together, and we always will be.
You won't give up poetry, and I won't let myself be
your subject matter. I'm leaving now. I have a cab waiting outside. There's no point even in telling you where
I'm going. I've packed everything. There's nothing that
will have to be forwarded."

He had dropped his hands from her shoulders and
stepped back. "You're carrying the matter too far, Miranda. That dumb leprechaun put a lot of wrong ideas
in your head. I didn't choose my poetry over you. Such
a thing would never occur to me." When her expression
didn't change, he added with cold correctness, "But it's
as you wish, of course." He opened the door for her and
carried her bag to the waiting taxi. Then with a polite,
"I hope you have a pleasant journey, Miranda," he closed
the car door. His face was starkly white under the street
lamp, his nostrils pinched with stubborn pride, his mouth
straight as a drawn sword.

As Miranda settled back in the taxi, there was a cold,
hard lump in the pit of her stomach. It would take her a
long time to get over Brian, longer than it had Craig.
The lump became an aggressive, punishing fist now,

doubled up inside her. What she had feared had come true. She had lost Brian. She, Miranda Dunn, was now a two-time loser, a woman with a losing track record in love. No matter that it was she who had done the walking out. The score was the same.

Chapter Ten

As THE TAXI neared Dublin's airport, Miranda wondered if she shouldn't have planned to return to Killarney instead of going to London. But too many questions—from the Royces and others—would have awaited her in Killarney, whereas Barbara, Miranda told herself wryly, would probably not only cheer her on but also undoubtedly try to find a substitute for Brian. Besides, she still had a week of vacation left and what could she do with it in Killarney?

Miranda's anger ebbed during the wait for her London flight. A feeling of melancholy set in, and she began to wonder if she hadn't overreacted to the situation. She bought a slab of chocolate for comfort but gave up on it because her unshed tears had caused a lump as big and hard as a golf ball to form in her throat.

Her depression deepened when her seat mate on the plane turned out to be a red-faced, hard-breathing businessman who reeked of gin and fumbled in her lap on the excuse that he was trying to help her with her seat belt. Miranda fended him off successfully, but even so it was a relief when the plane landed.

Heathrow was in its usual state of organized chaos. People of every nationality and race in the world seemed to be there—Indian women in bright saris, a formation of Japanese tourists, black-veiled Arab women, Americans streaming into the duty-free shop for cashmeres and cameras and Scotch, and English families returning from California vacations, the kids in Mickey Mouse hats, their parents sporting sheriffs' badges and bolo ties.

Miranda's spirits lifted a little in the shiny black London cab she took from the airport to Barbara's flat in Kensington. Looking out the window, it struck her that the city, which she had visited so often, was like an old friend. Its windows sparkled; white woodwork and black wrought-iron grillwork were glossy as wet paint; and the old, worn brick spoke of survival and endurance and permanent values.

When the cab stopped in front of Barbara's remodeled red-brick Edwardian building, Miranda paid the driver with the English pounds she had gotten at the Heathrow branch of a London bank. The driver took her generous tip with a broad smile and an enthusiastic "Ta, miss," and drove off, the blue light atop his cab glowing ghostily in the dark.

Miranda turned and looked at the house. Three broad, shallow steps flanked by two fat marble pillars led up to polished mahogany double doors with shiny brass knockers. There were begonia-filled flowerpots at the tall, narrow, ground-floor windows, and lace curtains shrouded all the windows. A line of silvery aluminum posts on the sidewalk of the narrow street prevented drivers from parking there.

Miranda had phoned Barbara from Ireland. She hadn't told her friend the reason for her sudden visit, but Barbara's worried face as she opened the door showed she had guessed from Miranda's muted tones that something was wrong. However, Barbara was too polite to pry and concentrated immediately on making Miranda comfortable in her modern little flat. But, Miranda thought, you can't drink midnight cocoa in your friend's kitchen, the two of you in bathrobe and pajamas, without, in effect, letting down your hair.

"You're a doll to take me in on such short notice," she said to her friend.

"Nonsense," Barbara answered brusquely. "And stop sniffling into your cocoa; it ruins the taste. You can stay as long as you like. I have no intention of paying the slightest attention to you—I have my own pathetic life to lead. I won't even ask what happened between you and Ireland's most passionate poet."

"We broke up." Miranda tried to keep a woeful note out of her voice, but it was there all the same.

"Really! Is that all? My pet, you are looking at a woman with more broken relationships in her past than a nineteenth-century courtesan."

Miranda laughed weakly. Then, in an attempt to avoid the egotism of her own unhappiness, she asked, "How's Colin?"

"Who?" Barbara's light blue eyes gleamed with the mischief of her own joke.

"Barbara, you're incorrigible—but probably right in your attitude toward men. They're not worth being serious about."

"A lot of them aren't, but your Brian *is* worth caring about, and the two of you are obviously good together." Barbara looked down into her empty cup. "Unless I'm misreading these cocoa dregs, you and he are headed for a long, lovely marriage, and I insist on being godmother to your first child, who will probably be spouting chemical formulas in rhymed couplets by the time he's five."

"You too, Brutus?" Miranda said bitterly.

"The name's *Barbara*," her friend answered dryly. "What's got into you? You don't seem a bit like yourself."

"Oh, nothing, just that people who don't believe in marriage and people who don't think I should marry anyone but a scientist are now urging me in no uncertain terms to marry Brian O'Bannon, Ireland's leading blarneyer, betrayer, and all around bastard."

Barbara leaned her elbows on the table and surveyed Miranda with a smug smile. "Umm. As bad as all that, eh? And you're never going to see him again, and if he calls I'm not supposed to tell him you're here?"

"I know you're being coy and cute and sardonic, Barbara, but I'm ignoring it, and yes, if he calls don't tell him I'm here. But he won't call. We're really finished. It's actually all for the best," Miranda said earnestly. "We're basically incompatible, and it's better to discover it now than later."

"The way you two were cavorting around Killarney's lakes and dells didn't look like incompatibility to me. Now in the interest of our getting to bed sometime tonight, would you mind telling me what happened between you and Brian?"

Miranda told her friend about the poetry reading.

Barbara listened attentively, her face a mask until Miranda had finished. "I can understand your feeling like that, Miranda. The English are supposed to value privacy highly, but when I used to visit you during school holidays and when we were roomies in Boston, I thought you were the most private person I had ever known— *anywhere*. It was a long time before you could confide in me or shared any of your feelings."

"I never knew you felt that way, Barb. Did it bother you?"

"Not when I understood what caused it."

"If you're going to say something against Frazier,

forget it. He's my father, after all."

"Not *against* him; *about* him—and the probable effect on you."

Miranda got up suddenly. "I want more cocoa. Where do you keep the stuff?" Barbara pointed to a cabinet, and Miranda plugged in the electric tea kettle before taking the tin of cocoa out. With her back to the wall, Miranda said, "Frazier couldn't help it. He wanted so much for me, he thought he had a right to pry, although I'm sure he didn't see it as prying. He believed that it was in my best interest—so he could guide me—to know what I thought, how I was doing in school, where my strengths and weaknesses lay, who my friends were, and if they were good enough for me. And as a result..."

"You closed in on yourself like an oyster, intimacy being the pearl inside the shell."

"Very poetic, Barb. Maybe *you* should write poetry."

Barbara grinned. "I do, but it's no good."

"A geneticist writing poetry?" Miranda wrinkled her nose in surprise.

"That's *why*. I need some outlet for my imagination, feeble as it may be."

The kettle whistled. Miranda made two cups of instant cocoa and carried them to the table. "So you think I overreacted to Brian's poem?"

"Knowing you, I'd say it's highly likely."

"I'm not sure. Maybe I'm stubborn, but I just can't bring myself to the point of accepting that—going public with one's lovemaking."

"Stubborn? Oh no, you're not stubborn," Barbara said airily. "Not the woman who sat on a lab stool eight solid hours trying to make a computation come out right. Now drink your cocoa like a good girl and let's go to bed, or I'll have more circles under my eyes than a tree has rings."

For the next few days, Miranda tidied up the flat every

morning after Barbara left for work and then embarked on a frenzied program of busyness. She went to the Science Museum in South Kensington and looked at reconstructions of early and modern chemistry laboratories. Then she crossed the street to the Natural History Museum and wandered through the Whale Hall, with its models and skeletons of whales and dolphins. Next she visited the "V and A," the Victoria and Albert Museum, and looked at the Constable paintings there. Methodically, she covered the British Museum, the Tate Gallery, Madame Tussaud's, and the Tower of London.

"But surely you've seen those museums before," Barbara said.

Miranda admitted flatly that she had, but explained that museum-hopping gave her something to do.

She walked a lot, too—through nearby Kensington Gardens and on to Hyde Park; then to Green Park, where the pale autumn sun glanced through the yellowing leaves of the plane trees. Straight ahead lay Buckingham Palace and to the left St. James Park; there, she stood on a little bridge and watched a flotilla of snowy white pelicans breast an algae-green lake.

The places she went—the parks, the museums, the monuments, and the exquisite Wren churches—were just stopping places for her body—anchors to the outside world. Her inner life was far more important, and that was taken up with an agonizing search for answers. Had she overreacted to Brian's poem "Illuminations"? Was she, as Barbara had said, too private a person? Was she perhaps even incapable of love? The last possibility she dismissed immediately; but she also felt strongly that, right or wrong, the stance she had taken was the only one possible. The idea of any part of her life being put on public display was absolute anathema to her.

* * *

Miranda and Barbara frequently ate supper in a little wine bar in the neighborhood. A candle stuck in a wine bottle lit each small, polished wood table. Rows of wine bottles adorned the bar. The day's specials—beef chasseur with rice, and spinach lasagna—were chalked on a blackboard propped against a wall. The crowd was young. Many, seemingly, came from nearby offices, and the persistent beat of rock music throbbed above the high-pitched chatter.

"I called Killarney today to let Walter Royce know where I was," Miranda said one evening, warming a glass of Beaujolais between her hands. "He doesn't need me, but he's heard from Frazier. My dad's due in Killarney within the week, so I'll be taking off soon."

"Really! Without seeing the Regent's Park Zoo?" Barbara asked ironically. "And how about the Horniman Museum? You missed that one, too."

"Would you rather I had moped around the house?"

"What's the difference whether you mope in public or in private?"

"Actually, I was thinking . . . trying to figure out whether I had been unfair to Brian."

"You could have saved your time, my pet, and asked old Auntie Barbara."

"Okay, I'm asking now."

"In a word, yes, you were unfair. Brian would never do anything to hurt you. Nobody even knows who a poet has written about until the poor dear is dead and the culture vultures go to work on his biography. Brian loves you and you love him, and that's the most beautiful thing in the world." Barbara raised her voice in tremulous song on the last words, and a man sitting alone lifted his glass to her. She acknowledged the salute with a smile, then turned her attention back to Miranda. "Someone once said, 'Life is like learning to play the violin and giving a concert at the same time.' I'm all for privacy, but there's a limit to it, like anything else. Besides"—Barbara looked around the room conspiratorially and lowered her voice—"Brian's in London."

Miranda's heart leaped into her throat. It was a second or two before she could speak, and then words came in a burst of staccato questions. "How do you know? Does he know where I am? Did you tell him?"

"Yes. He called me from Dublin and asked, and I told him you were staying with me."

Miranda flushed with indignation. "Thanks a lot. I asked you not to."

"How are you two ever going to make up if you don't see each other?" Barbara complained. She was openly responding now to the man's gestured invitation, miming elaborately that it was Miranda's presence alone that was preventing her from accepting it.

Suddenly sickened by Barbara's betrayal of her confidence and her behavior in the wine bar, Miranda rose. "I'm going home. Are you coming, or do you have a big evening planned?" She darted a disgusted glance at the man sitting nearby.

Barbara smiled in what Miranda thought was a particularly smug way. "Run along, my pet. I'll see you later."

Miranda strode along Kensington High Street, her hands in her suit jacket pockets for warmth against the stiff evening breeze. She passed a street vendor selling chestnuts roasted in a brazier whose coals glowed red in the dark night, and she doubled back to buy a bag. She divided the contents between her pockets to keep her hands warm and continued her brisk walk to the flat. As she unlocked the door with the key Barbara had given her, she wondered why the lights were on. In a sudden flash of insight, she conjectured that Barbara had arranged to have Brian and her meet. If Barbara hadn't accepted the solitary man's invitation to drink with him,

she would undoubtedly have found some other pretext
to leave Miranda alone with Brian. Yet suddenly Miranda
felt her heart beat joyously at the prospect of seeing Brian
again. Lord, how she had missed him, and perhaps she
had been unreasonable ...

A man in a tweed jacket was standing at the window,
his back to Miranda.

She called "Brian!" and took a long step toward him,
but he was the wrong size and his hair was light, and
suddenly Miranda was afraid.

He turned around, and her fear abated somewhat.
Whoever he was, he had a good-humored face, with long,
angular features that made him look a bit like an amiable
horse. "Hullo," he said, "I'm Colin. Where's Barbara?"

Miranda collected her wits enough not to stammer
what came into her mind, that Barbara was sitting at a
round wooden table in a wine bar, drinking with a perfect
stranger and apparently not through any altruistic motive
of bringing lovers together, either. "I'm Miranda Dunn.
Barbara probably mentioned me."

"Of course. Barbara ran off to you in Killarney when
we had our little blow-up."

"And I"—Miranda swallowed hard and forced herself
to say what she had in mind—"have run off to Barbara
after *my* little blow-up." She laughed, partly to show that
it was a half-joking statement and partly out of relief that
she had succeeded in a personal admission she could
never have made before.

Colin grinned. "I know. The Irish poet. He phoned
you, by the way."

"He did?" Completely taken aback by Colin's cool
delivery of this stupendous piece of news, Miranda could
only stare wide-eyed at him.

"His name's Brian O'Bannon, right?"

Miranda nodded.

"Well, he rang up about half an hour ago and asked

for you. When I told him both you and Barbara were
out, he requested that you give him a ring when you get
back." Colin ambled toward the telephone. "He left a
number. I jotted it down." He handed a piece of paper
to Miranda. "Here it is."

Miranda looked down at the number scrawled on the
paper. It seemed almost miraculous that in just a few
minutes seven digits would transform her life. She would
hear Brian's warm voice, its strength softened by the hint
of a Kerry lilt, and this time they wouldn't speak cold,
angry words to each other. All those dreary hours of
tramping around London had produced a change in her
that she could hardly wait to tell him about. Her heart
bounding with joy, Miranda lifted the receiver. At the
same time, she heard a key being turned in the lock.

"Miranda! Brian! It's me. I've given you two all the
time I can. I'm blue with cold from walking Kensington
High Street. Besides, I'm a working girl and have to get
up—" Barbara broke off and stopped on the threshold
of the living room. "Colin!" A look of joy followed the
surprise on her face. "What are you doing back?"

"I came for the leather sandals I bought when we were
in Spain. I left them behind. Also, I thought..."

"Yes?" Barbara interrupted eagerly.

A somewhat embarrassed grin spread across Colin's
bony face. "I thought you might be glad to see me."

"Two weeks *is* a long time," Barbara said coolly, but
as she moved across the room toward Colin, Miranda
noticed her pleased look and didn't doubt that Colin did,
too. "You *do* take our little tiffs seriously, don't you?"

The telephone receiver in her hand, Miranda turned
away from the embrace that was obviously taking place.
This seemed to be Lovers' Reconciliation Night. She felt
guilty about having misconstrued Barbara's behavior in
the wine bar. Obviously, Barbara had expected Brian to
be here. Miranda could have cried with disappointment

when the figure at the window turned out to be Colin, but if Brian had been delayed or prevented from coming, it wasn't crucial; they would simply make a date for another time.

She dialed the number Colin had taken down and listened to the familiar double ring—*burr-burr* . . . pause . . . *burr-burr*. She let it ring for a long time and was aware that Colin and Barbara were waiting, too. When, finally, she put the phone down, she was acutely disappointed and puzzled. Why, if he cared about her, hadn't he waited for her call? For the first time since Colin told her Brian had phoned, she realized that it might have been to bid her a final good-bye, to tell her that all was definitely over between them. In that case, of course he wouldn't be eagerly awaiting her call.

"He probably just stepped out for a pack of cigarettes," Barbara said in a comforting voice.

"You know he doesn't smoke," Miranda answered glumly. "In the arrangements you and he made," she continued in a dry tone, "was he supposed to come here?"

"Yes. I even met him for lunch so I could give him a key. He wanted to surprise you. Something probably prevented him from coming and that's what he called to tell you."

"Right," Miranda replied sarcastically. "And he was so upset about it, he sat around waiting for me to return his call." She rose from the chair by the telephone. "It doesn't matter," she added briskly. "I'll try again tomorrow." She said good night and went to her room. A short time later, she heard Colin leave, but she was sure he would be back the next day or soon thereafter. Barbara was luckier in love than she was.

The next day Miranda dialed the number Colin had given her, but she did so with great reluctance. It had to be the acme of duty, she mused, to call the man you love so that he could dump you, for this was surely the reason Brian had called her and now was ducking her return call; he had lost his nerve at the last moment. This time when there was no answer, she was relieved.

"Perhaps he was unexpectedly called away," Barbara said. "Come to think about it, he did sound a bit mysterious, talking about some new venture he had on hand. Not to worry, my pet, I'm sure he'll call again today. Colin's coming by to take me to a little gallery he's discovered in Chelsea. Would you like to come with us, or do you think you should do the patience-on-a-monument thing by the telephone? You know, Shakespeare. 'She never told her love' ... blah ... blah ... 'And with a green and yellow melancholy,/She sat like Patience on a monument,/Smiling at grief.'"

"Bravo!" Colin had walked in and stood in front of the two women, applauding. "Viola's speech to the duke, act four, scene two of *Twelfth Night* by William Shakespeare."

Barbara wrinkled her short, classically shaped nose. "Act four? It's been a long time since school, but I think Viola says that earlier on."

"Did I say act four? I meant act two, *scene* four! I have a terrible habit of transposing numbers," he confessed ruefully. "Luckily, numbers aren't important in my line of work."

"Colin works for the Foreign Office, and not even *I* know what he does," Barbara said. After a moment's thoughtful silence, shared by Colin and Miranda, Barbara screamed, "Colin, you twit! You transposed the digits in Brian's number!"

"It's possible," Colin admitted shamefacedly. "There wasn't a pencil by the phone, so I had to remember the number until I could find one. Then I had to hunt up a scrap of paper to write it on."

They fell silent again. All Miranda could think was, He's somewhere in London, one of seven million people, and he's sure now I don't love him because I didn't call him back.

Chapter Eleven

"CAN'T YOU REMEMBER the number *at all*, Colin?" Barbara probed impatiently.

Colin shook his head, his expression so woebegone that Miranda couldn't help but feel sorry for him. Then, briskly, with newfound purpose, he said, "I'll try a few combinations of the digits." But the first phone call reached a Chinese "take-away" and the second an irate night watchman who slept days and called Colin a "blithering idiot" for dialing the wrong number.

Several unsuccessful phone calls later, Colin said, "There's no use trying anymore. I have such a poor memory for figures, I might have gotten most of O'Bannon's phone number wrong. There *is* a way out, though."

"I would hope so," Barbara said sarcastically, "or what's the Foreign Office for?"

Turning to Miranda and ignoring Barbara's acid comment, Colin continued, "Put an announcement in the personal column of *The Times*, why don't you? Something like 'Won't you come home, Brian O'Bannon. I miss you all the time. Miranda.'"

"I couldn't do a thing like that, Colin."

"Why not? You're not going to reach him by telephone, that's obvious. You're hardly likely to bump into him on the Strand. He undoubtedly reads *The Times;* I mean, everyone does. It's your only way."

"But it's so *public!*" Miranda said with distaste. She caught Barbara's sardonic stare and guessed what she was thinking—*Miranda would rather give up the man she loves than her precious privacy.* "All right, I'll do it," Miranda said spiritedly. "But won't it take a couple of days for the notice to appear, Colin?"

He replied, "If you get it in by one-thirty, it will be in tomorrow's paper."

With a withering look at Colin, Barbara said, "It's past two now."

Colin winked. "Not to worry. I have a friend in the appropriate department."

"Colin, you're an angel!" Barbara cried.

"That's what I've been waiting to hear."

"Wait a minute. Who's your friend 'in the appropriate department'?" Barbara asked, suddenly haughty and hot-eyed with jealousy.

A happy, somewhat smug expression softened Colin's bony face. "I wanted to hear *that* even more." He turned to Miranda. "Write up your notice for the personals, Miranda, and I'll phone it in for you."

Thanks to Colin, the notice—BRIAN. PLEASE CALL AGAIN. MIRANDA—appeared the very next day, and the day after that, to keep her mind off the telephone, Miranda scoured every pot and pan in Barbara's kitchen and washed and waxed the vinyl floor. Reverting to the schoolgirl superstition that if you think you'll fail an exam, you're sure to pass, she told herself that Brian wouldn't call. And even when the familiar *burr-burr* of the phone sounded, she prepared herself for Barbara or Colin's voice.

The result was that when she heard Brian's soft "Miranda?" she could only stand mute with the phone in her hand.

Then the terrible thought struck her that, believing he had got the wrong number or she had changed her mind, he might hang up, so she stammered in a hurried staccato, "Yes, it's me, Miranda. Colin transposed the digits in your telephone number; that's why I couldn't call you back. Brian, are you still there?"

"Yes, love, I am."

She could hear the joyful laughter brimming up under his words. He knows that I love him, Miranda thought, and she thrilled to being a woman openly and obviously in love.

"I'm sorry about the other night," he continued. "Something urgent came up, and I couldn't get to Barbara's flat. I'll tell you about it when I see you. Shall I come now and carry you off?"

"Yes, do. I'll pack and leave a note for Barbara. But where will we go?"

"I know an exquisite little cottage in the Cotswolds that we can rent. Would that please you?"

Miranda told him it would please her very much, then she hung up the telephone gently, as though afraid to jar their reconciliation. As she packed and got ready for him, all her motions seemed to take on a new, graceful fluidity, as though she were finally in harmony with herself and the world outside.

Too full of happiness to say much, Miranda and Brian settled into the little two-seater he had rented and started on their hundred-mile trip to the gently molded Cotswold Hills in southcentral England.

Miranda wore a brown tweed jacket and gold corduroy

skirt to match the autumnal colors of the countryside they drove through. Putting her arm next to Brian's similarly clad one, she said, "We're twins—Tweedledum and Tweedledee."

"You're fairly literary for a scientist who insists she isn't," Brian said with a sidelong smile.

"I had a good general education before I narrowed my interests down to my specialty. Also," Miranda continued thoughtfully, "I feel freer somehow about literature and poetry—less defensive."

"Why is that, would you say?"

"I think I used to feel inferior because I didn't know a great deal about literature the way I did about biology, so I ended up being inhibited about using the knowledge I did have. Now I realize that although one can't be an expert in everything, one can enjoy a great many things one is not expert in."

Brian smiled a little smugly.

"I know what you're thinking, Brian O'Bannon, that you said it first when you told me life wasn't a matter of climbing ladders but of exploring rich labyrinths."

"Sure and a man can't be put in jail for his thoughts."

The ardent look he swept over her made Miranda say dryly, "I wonder. At any rate," she continued, "let's not quarrel about 'Illuminations' again, Brian. I may have been wrong—I'm not saying I wasn't—but I honestly couldn't have reacted any other way."

"I blame myself for not having realized how you felt. I promise you, Miranda, I won't celebrate our love in my poetry again."

"I might change in time," she conceded. "Then you could."

"Could what?" he asked, his cobalt-blue eyes wide with simulated innocence.

"Celebrate our love," she answered, a little shyly.

"That's what I'm planning on, *macushla,* but not in

poetry." Their lane of traffic had been stopped temporarily for road repairs, and now his long look of physical desire made love-promises to parts of her body that were like a magic wand, calling up from deep within her a throbbing response of excitement and yearning for him.

They reached the cottage late in the afternoon, when the setting sun cast a mellow light over the fields of golden stubble and warmed the stone of the village houses to the color of honey. The cottage stood alone beyond the quiet, curving street of the village. An oak tree and an immense copper beech shaded it a little too well for the cool days of autumn, Miranda thought, but Brian soon had a roaring fire going and the cottage began to lose its dampness.

He drew her in his arms and whispered with his cheek against hers, "There's a historic inn in the village if you're hungry."

She wound her arms around his neck and rubbed her nose against his. "I'd rather we made our own history."

He stopped her with a gentle hand on her chin. "Pretty outspoken, aren't you?"

She removed his hand so she could nuzzle him some more. "Don't forget I'm a biologist. I know things about the birds and the bees you never even dreamed of." She dropped her mouth to his then and kissed him with warm, moist sweetness.

When the kiss finally ended, Brian said, "That's what I like—aggressive women."

"*Passive*-aggressive," Miranda corrected, flinging herself onto the couch in front of the fire, arms outstretched, eyes closed.

"You look like a Victorian maiden waiting to be ravished," Brian said, looking down at her.

Miranda opened her eyes, glanced at her watch, and said, "So—when?"

He narrowed his eyes and his gaze drifted along her

prone body as though he were making plans. But what plans? Miranda's nerves tingled with expectation as she waited for his embrace. He dropped to his knees beside her and took her face firmly between both his hands. Slowly, carefully, as if every feature were precious to him, he planted a kiss on her full eyelids and the diagonal of her cheekbones and her nose and the tip of her chin. Miranda never felt more tenderly loved than she did then.

"I want to love you all over," he said huskily, "to make up for those blasted nights when we were apart, when I was practically out of my mind with fear that you wouldn't come back to me."

"I couldn't have stayed away. Don't you know that, darling?" Miranda caught her breath in a sharp, ecstatic cry, for Brian had slipped his hand up under her sweater, brushing her breast with an electrifying sweep of his fingers. He pulled her sweater off and peeled down the lacy cups of her bra. He gazed for a moment at the ripe glory of her smooth, mounding breasts; then, with a deep groan, he thrust his face against them, caressing them with the sharp stubble of his cheek, playfully rubbing his nose against a nipple, then taking it in his mouth, applying only so much pressure as would permit her to feel the soft scrape of his teeth as he gently tugged.

Miranda raked her fingers through his thick dark hair and had to remind herself not to pull hard, as his mouth excited her more and more.

"I adore you, Miranda," Brian whispered. "I love the little hollow at the point of your collarbone, and the way your beautiful breasts rise out of your slenderness like fruits on a vine, and your high-arched, sexy little feet."

"I don't call a *seven* exactly little," Miranda remonstrated, arching her back to help him as he put his hands under her skirt and pulled down her panty hose.

"Ssh, don't argue, woman," he murmured, taking her foot in his hand and running kisses along its high instep.

An almost unbearably delicious thrill, like a honey-tipped spear, seemed to plunge to the very core of her. And when he took each toe in his mouth and delicately sucked it, Miranda moaned in ecstasy.

Then she attempted to wrestle with his clothes, but feverishly, he did the job himself, tearing at the buttons impatiently until finally he stood before her, the muscles rippling in his arms, his chest matted with a dark pelt, his bold sex strongly outlined under his white briefs.

Muttering, "I always finish what I start," he slid her skirt down over her hips. "Now we're even," he said with a grin as he kissed the soft flesh just above the line of her lacy bikinis. He scooped her off the couch then and held her in his arms, their bodies, rosy-hued from the fire, pressed close together.

"We look like a Rubens," Miranda said gleefully.

"Venus and Adonis," Brian breathed, planting a last tantalizing kiss on one eager nipple before carrying her to the bedroom. There, he set her gently down on the bed and slipped his hands inside her panties, easing them off her with exquisite, torturing slowness, as his fingers explored and touched and loved her. To get even, Miranda tried to remove his white cotton briefs with the same arousing lack of speed. But his control was less sure than hers and with a moaned *"Macushla, my heart's joy,"* he covered her and filled her with all of himself. In her rapture as their passion carried her further and further beyond herself, Miranda knew a moment of transcendence and of more than physical union with Brian. The magic of love, she thought, was that it made one and one equal *one*, not two.

Afterward, as she lay in his arms, Miranda told Brian how she had felt. "It was the same way for me, *macushla*," he whispered against her moist hair. "Marry me, Miranda. It won't be at all like what it was with Craig. I'll be no cool colleague of the bedroom or anywhere else, I assure you."

As Miranda, her emotions tumultuous, remained silent, he continued, "I have a bit of news for you. I've been keeping it back to surprise you. A New York publisher is interested in having me expand my lectures on poetry and science into a book."

"That's terrific, Brian. Is that the new venture you told Barbara you were working on?"

Brian nodded, smiling. "We could collaborate on it. It would be our first venture as husband and wife." He gave her a little squeeze, thereby setting bells ringing in her again. "What do you say, *macushla?*"

"I need a little time to think. It's the way I am, Brian.' I can't do things impulsively." That was true as far as it went, but was there more? She still hadn't told Brian about her fellowship or shared with him the nagging fear that for some unknown reason this marriage might not work out, just as her marriage to Craig hadn't. "Besides, I have to go back to Killarney."

"I thought you had a few days left of your vacation."

"I do, but my father will be arriving in Killarney tomorrow, and it wouldn't be right if I wasn't there when he came. Will you come? I would like you to meet him."

"Of course. I plan to ask him for his daughter's hand, now that I have her body."

Laughing, he pulled her down on top of him, and her vague sense of dread about the decisions she soon would have to make disappeared in the joy of their love.

Chapter Twelve

FRAZIER DUNN'S PLANS were to rent a car at Shannon Airport and drive to Killarney. Miranda spotted the unfamiliar English Ford as soon as the taxi she and Brian had taken at the Killarney train station on the last leg of their journey from London drew up in front of her house.

"My father's here. Come in and meet him now," Miranda coaxed.

"It's been a while since you've seen your dad. Why don't you spend some time alone with him first? I'll see you both tonight at the party the Royces are giving for him." He kissed her lightly on the lips. Like soft, winy grapes, her lips clung to his, and his kiss deepened for a moment. Then he pulled away. "You'd best go now, *macushla;* but when we're married, so help me, there'll never be a kiss we don't complete."

The cabby helped Miranda with her bag, and her father came to the door to meet her as she entered the house. The quick exchange of cool, cheek-brushing kisses over, they stepped back to look at each other. Miranda noted that Frazier had retained his slim, wiry build and flat stomach, an achievement at his age, which she knew he owed to disciplined exercise and diet. Discipline was the hallmark of his face, too—the iron-gray hair, cut considerably shorter than was fashionable; the chestnut-colored eyes, always alert, observing, judging; and the tightly controlled mouth.

And how did her father see her? Miranda's hand went to her lips, which still glowed from Brian's kiss, then touched her cheek. I'm kiss-bruised and flushed and exude fulfillment, she thought. My eyes sparkle, my steps are quick and light, and I feel like throwing my arms around anyone who'll let me. I'm a walking advertisement for love, and he sees it.

"I found the key where your letter said it would be." Frazier eyed Miranda's suitcase. "You didn't tell me where you were going." His voice was cold and dry; his face bleached of expression as his eyes took note of her appearance.

Miranda took a deep breath before answering. "I've been away on vacation with a friend—my lover," she added, holding his eyes with her own.

As she expected, Frazier uttered a discreet little cough, smiled uncomfortably, and promptly changed the subject. His face alive with interest now, he asked, "Have you heard from the Wolcott Institute?"

"I got the fellowship," Miranda said flatly.

Frazier took a few excited steps back and forth. "Wonderful! I knew you would. Yet there's so much competition in the field, one can never be entirely sure. This will make your career, Miranda. You'll be working under some of the best people in the country."

"I may not accept the fellowship, Frazier," Miranda said slowly, watching his face, waiting first for astonishment, then for the familiar look of mingled disappointment and disapproval to cross his chiseled features.

I've been here before, Miranda thought. I had just handed him a less than perfect report card and stood waiting for his reaction. I wanted to say "Dad" instead of the "Frazier" he insisted I call him, and I wished he would scold me, yell at me—do anything but give me "the look," as I called it—then tell me he loved me no matter what grades I got. But being Frazier Dunn, he couldn't, I suppose. Instead, his eyes held such contempt that I vowed I would never do anything to provoke that look again. And I haven't—until now.

"May I ask why you've arrived at this bizarre decision, Miranda?" He had stepped back from her, and his expression as he observed her was one of detached objectivity.

"I've fallen in love with an Irishman who lives here in Killarney. He's asked me to marry him; he's the one I've been on vacation with. I haven't said yes yet, and I haven't told him about the fellowship because I wanted time to think. My job here is a good one. I may simply stay on. Or . . ." Miranda waved her hand vaguely in the air.

"Or have him come to New York with you," Frazier interrupted eagerly. "Why not, Miranda? You haven't told me what his field is, but with my connections I'm sure I could place him in one of the research facilities in the New York area."

"He's not a scientist, Frazier."

"Oh?" Her father's thin dark eyebrows shot up in surprise. "What *does* he do, then?"

"He's a poet," Miranda said quietly.

"A poet!" A look of distaste crossed Frazier's face. "Really, Miranda, you can't be serious. Next you'll be telling me you believe in fairies."

Miranda couldn't help herself. Her dark eyes pranced with glee. "They're called the gentry here, Frazier, because if you don't treat them with respect, they're apt to do you a bad turn."

"Don't be childish, Miranda!" That too evoked memories—of the many times when as a child she had been admonished for behaving "childishly." "How did you come in contact with this man, anyway?"

"You make him sound like a disease I caught," Miranda said dryly. "Brian is one of the foremost poets of Ireland—of the world. His last name is O'Bannon. Brian O'Bannon." Some streak of perversity made her add, "Perhaps you've heard of him."

Her father shot her a look of utter disbelief.

"Walter Royce arranged to have Brian give a series of lectures on poetry and science at Biochem, and I helped Brian. I may also collaborate with him on a book that will be an extension of his lectures."

Frazier relaxed visibly. "Oh, that's it. The fellow wants your name on his book and your help—for nothing, of course."

"Hardly!" Miranda said indignantly. "He's proposed that we marry."

"Why, of course—so you can produce more books together, or so eventually he can live off your salary while he composes his drivel. Poets belong to that group of hypocrites who make themselves out to be more idealistic than the rest of us poor misguided mortals. But the fact that this O'Bannion—or whatever his name is—wants to use the lectures Walter let him give for a book he'll make money from and use *you* in the bargain to help him shows he's just as ambitious and materialistic as anyone else. He fed you a line of blarney, and you fell for it. Although how *you*—as intelligent as you are—could have, I really don't know, Miranda."

As though it were the stimulus to a conditioned reflex, her father's *blarney* triggered a wave of panic in Miranda. There was no denying Brian's mastery of language; his charm; his ability, if he chose to use it, to induce people to do what he wanted. Was Frazier right? By Brian's own admission, poetry books didn't sell well, but a more far-reaching book on poetry and science might. Was Brian, after all, interested in scaling ladders, especially with Miranda at his side to supply the rungs?

"Well," Miranda said brightly in a quick change of subject, "I'm not much of a hostess, am I? Let me show you to your room, and then you must tell me about Mom and what she's been up to. I'll make lunch while you freshen up. You'll meet Brian tonight at Walter and Janet's party for you. I'm sure you'll change your mind about him once you get to know him," Miranda added gravely.

Frazier smiled condescendingly at her and shook his head slowly, as at one besotted by love. Then he picked up his suitcase and stood aside for Miranda to lead the way to the spare bedroom.

Miranda dressed carefully for the party. Frazier liked a well-turned-out woman, and her pride demanded that he see her as such. She hoped, too, that looking her best would give her the confidence and courage she would need for the crisis she sensed was coming. And so, she chose a black georgette chemise she had bought in London. It had long sleeves and was perfectly simple except for the dramatic low-cut V neck edged with gold beading and sequins, repeated on the shoulders. She swept her hair up into a French roll and wore large black and gold butterfly earrings. Very sheer black hose and high-heeled black sandals completed the sophisticated impression she wanted to create. Her evening makeup gave her a sultrier look than she had intended, but she wasn't dressing just for her father, was she? Her lover would be at the party.

Frazier and Miranda arrived early. The hired bartender was arranging green olives and slices of lemon in crystal dishes; Mary and her "temps" were placing pink linen napkins, swirled like cotton candy, on the buffet table;

and Janet was making a final inspection of the party preparations with the calm of an experienced hostess who knows that everything has been done and an inspection really isn't necessary.

"I'm glad you came early," Walter said, greeting them. "Janet's got everything so well organized, there isn't a damn thing for me to do but practice my smile."

Frazier laughed and clapped Walter on the shoulder. "I'm not hanging around to be smiled at by an old rascal like you. I'm looking for someone a lot prettier. Janet! You're the one I want to see. I listened to all Walt's tall fish stories this morning, but I haven't had a chance to talk to you." He met a smiling Janet halfway and exchanged a friendly hug and kiss with her. Then, with his arm lightly around her shoulders, he drew her away from Walter and Miranda.

"You look terrific tonight, Miranda," Walter said. "If I were twenty years younger and an Irish poet . . . by the way, I've been asked to write the introduction to Brian's book on poetry and science, and in the course of my conversation with the publisher, I learned something very interesting about Brian. Did you know . . ." Walter stopped at the sound of the doorbell. "Tell you later," he said with a smile, leaving Miranda to go to the door.

After a while, Walter left the door open to the autumn night and the guests who were streaming in. Miranda didn't see Brian enter, and the first sight of him in the crowded living room gave her a shock crazily compounded of recognition and love and happiness. Then, touched and amused by the pains he had taken with his appearance, she turned her head away to hide a smile.

Brian looked glossy and ruddy and handsome as always, but tonight everything—shoes and socks, jacket and trousers–matched, his shirt collar was stiff, his tie straight, and his breast pocket was adorned with a crisp white point of Irish linen. The thought that he had done this for *her*, to impress *her* father, made Miranda's eyes shine with love. She threaded her way through the cocktail crowd and slipped her arm through his. "You look awfully handsome tonight, darling," she purred.

Brian turned, and the glow of happiness that lit his face as he saw her made Miranda's heart dance. "And *you* are an absolute knockout, Dr. Dunn." He leaned forward and whispered in her ear, "But I still prefer you as 'Nature Girl.'"

The brush of his lips across the delicate shell of her ear sent a tremor of excitement through Miranda. She felt herself go boneless and soft inside, and her hot blood rushed to the surface of her skin. A memory-hugging smile hovered at the corners of her mouth, and she narrowed her dark eyes for a moment at the thought of the joy that sooner or later would again be theirs.

But she had an uncanny sensation of being watched and opened her eyes to look into the stern, disapproving face of Frazier Dunn. He advanced the few steps that separated him from the couple, and Miranda said, "This is Brian O'Bannon, Frazier."

As the two men shook hands, Miranda noticed that her father's evaluating look, the prerogative of a man in a position of authority, was matched by Brian's quiet assessment of the older man. They exchanged a few joking banalities about the weather, then Frazier was captured by a newly arrived former colleague who wanted to talk shop with him.

"It's his party," Miranda said, laughing, as she and Brian watched a group form around her father. "I don't think there's anyone here he doesn't know, hasn't worked with at some time or other, or hasn't at least heard of. Frazier's quite a star in the scientific firmament, you know," she added with quiet pride.

"You call him Frazier?" Brian asked.

Miranda flushed. "Usually only when we're alone. I

used to call him that all the time, but I was ridiculed for it by other kids when I was young, so I stopped. He prefers it, and I respect his wish," she said simply.

"It makes you seem like colleagues, doesn't it?" Brian said in a neutral tone.

"I suppose so." Miranda thought she had never seen Brian's eyes look the way they did now—cautiously expressionless. "As I said, he was the one who wanted it, but it also helped me when I was preparing myself for a scientific career to see myself that way—as his colleague," Miranda said a little defensively.

Brian looked at her then with so much compassion that Miranda became angry. "Lay off the psychoanalyzing, will you please, Brian? I might have lost out on something in the relationship, but I gained a lot, too. I owe my career to Frazier—his interest in it, his fostering of my ambition, and his insistence that I develop the discipline to do the work."

A stubborn, stony look returned to Brian's face, and again Miranda fell prey to a feeling of foreboding. Brian and her father seemed to be headed for a clash. Moreover, although she had told Frazier that she might forgo the fellowship in favor of marrying Brian, she hadn't told Brian. Her lack of candor wasn't fair to him, but how could she tell Brian that she would marry him before she was sure? Miranda felt hemmed in by events that were moving faster than she wanted them to and decisions that were calling to be made before she was ready.

To blunt the impact of her angry words, Miranda said conversationally, "Walter has something interesting to tell me about your book—besides the fact that he's writing the introduction. It's something about you." She looked up at Brian archly. "The suspense is killing me. Would you care to tell me what Walter and your publisher know about you that I don't know?"

Brian grinned, and his eyes again sparkled like sunlit

water. "Much more interesting is what *you* know about me that Walter and my publisher don't."

With that, he escorted her to the buffet table, and Miranda didn't think until later that he had very nicely deflected her question. They found places for themselves and their plates of food at the top of the broad, carpeted stairs. Brian leaned his back against the polished oak banister and fed Miranda tidbits from his dish. "I feel like a trained poodle begging for my supper," she said with a laugh.

He took one of her hands in his and kissed it. "You have beautiful paws, Fifi." He rubbed his nose against hers. "And I adore your cold muzzle."

"Brian! People will see you."

"I certainly hope so," he said equably, holding out a miniature cornucopia of Irish ham and cheese to her. "I'd hate to be the Invisible Man. Think of the hours we'd waste unwinding all those bandages before I could make love to you. Speaking of which, when? Or more accurately, when again?"

"My father's leaving in two days. Could you come to lunch tomorrow? I'd like you two to know each other."

"I thought I was going to be asking him for your hand," Brian said dryly.

Miranda looked at him pleadingly. "I need time, Brian. I'm not sure yet."

Brian nodded curtly. His eyes had a flat, wary look in them again; but knowing him as she did, Miranda thought she could guess what he was thinking—that although she hadn't given him an answer, she had been sure about the two of them until Frazier arrived. Brian was right. Miranda despised herself for it, but she had been subtly infected, as by a pathogenic agent, by Frazier's attitude—both expressed and implicit—toward Brian. The old doubts about the possibility of compatibility between a poet and a scientist and about the future

of her career had resurfaced. In her mind, a slight miasmic
cloud had even settled over Brian's motives. But most
of all, she experienced a vague, unsettled dread of marriage itself. Irrational as it was, the conviction lurked
that she would fail again, and that this time the damage
to her life would be irreparable.

Chapter Thirteen

THE NEXT DAY, a Saturday, Miranda dressed with the same care for the luncheon she was giving for her father and Brian as she had for the Royces' cocktail buffet. Walter Royce had taken Frazier on a tour of Killarney, and Miranda had spent the morning cooking. As the entrée, Miranda had decided on fillet of Dover sole poached in white wine with mushrooms and garnished with oysters. It would be accompanied by a risotto and preceded by a simple green salad. She chose a white Burgundy for the wine, and her dessert, made early that morning, was a light sponge cake with an apricot glaze and slivered almonds.

The house tidied up, the table set, and the preliminary preparations for the luncheon made, Miranda stood in front of her mirror fingering the gold chain she had just put on. It complemented her ivory crepe de chine blouse nicely, but that wasn't what Miranda was thinking of.

She had slept badly during the night, awakened twice by the terror of nightmares. Finally, she had gotten up at five o'clock and made the sponge cake. From then until now, she'd hardly had a minute to think; but once she started to dress for the luncheon, her nervousness about the confrontation she expected between her father and Brian returned. The gold chain, put on merely as an ornament, had, strangely enough, calmed her.

Miranda had bought the necklace with money she had earned herself. Gifts of jewelry from men, even one's husband, had always been a little suspect to Miranda. It was an extreme view, she knew, but such gifts smacked to her of a reward for services rendered. Now, looking at herself in the mirror and at the gold chain lambent against the soft color of her blouse, Miranda reminded herself that she was an independent woman, that she had no control over the actions of either Frazier or Brian, and that whatever happened, she would survive.

Even so, Frazier's contemptuous "Has *your poet* arrived yet?" when Walter dropped him off at the door ruffled Miranda's calm.

"Why are you so antagonistic to him when you don't even know him?" she asked, her thin voice showing her tenseness.

"Because he's trying to take advantage of you. Can't you see that?"

"I don't believe he is, Frazier," she said steadily.

"Did he ask you to marry him before this book deal came along?"

"No, but it's a little farfetched to conjecture that that's the reason he wants to marry me, don't you think?"

"I didn't say it was the *only* reason. You're beautiful and brainy and will always be able to support yourself—and him. How much money do you think a poet makes, anyway? The would-be poets I knew in college—and don't think *they* weren't an arrogant bunch—*if* they stuck it out, ended up waiting on tables or driving cabs so they could eat. This book that O'Bannon is planning to have you write for him is going to be his bread and butter—and the first jam he's had in a long time, I'll bet."

As Miranda stood and stared at him, aghast at his vehemence, Frazier continued, "Walter likes him and so does Janet, but that doesn't mean anything. He's got charm, all right. I never said he didn't. That's how his kind always get along in the world—not through work, that's for sure."

So much of what Frazier was saying echoed what Miranda had thought about poets when she met Brian that she felt ashamed of her father and of herself.

Her distress must have shown on her face, because Frazier tried to comfort her with a stern, "Don't worry, Miranda, I'll get rid of this guy for you, and if he gives me any trouble I'll know how to handle that, too."

The doorbell rang then, and wide-eyed with alarm at Frazier's announcement of his intentions, Miranda went to the door. When Brian saw her, his strong features grew taut and his eyes turned a sea-cold blue she had never seen before. "Are you all right, *macushla?*" he asked in a low voice.

"Yes, of course, just a little tired from slaving over a hot stove all morning," she answered with a laugh. "Please come in. My father's here. He's just returned from a tour of Killarney with Walter."

The habits of good breeding smoothed over the meeting of the two men, and they exchanged the usual courtesies. Miranda served some cheese wafers she had baked and frozen weeks before, along with an apéritif, and after a while left the living room for the kitchen. Just before she was ready to put the salad on the table, she remembered that she had forgotten to uncork the white wine she planned to serve with the meal.

"Brian, will you open the wine for me, please?" she called out. She slid the baking dish containing the fish into the oven and turned to see not only Brian but her father standing behind her.

"I'm an old hand at this," Frazier said smoothly, reaching for the corkscrew.

With a nod, almost a little bow, Brian stepped back and answered politely, "Of course, sir."

"I don't suppose you get much call to open bottles of wine," Frazier continued as he pulled the cork out with a satisfying pop. "Whisky is more the thing here, isn't it?"

Miranda stared at him in horrified amazement. His tone was patronizing, attesting to the kind of condescending bonhomie used with social inferiors. She had never seen him behave like this. Demanding perfection of himself in everything, he had honed even the social graces to a fine point of old-fashioned courtesy.

A speculative, knowing look crossed Brian's face. He raised his eyebrows at the discourtesy shown him, but said nothing.

The reproof implicit in Brian's silence and the judgment in his cold, measuring gaze seemed to infuriate Frazier. He flushed as if he had been slapped and set his lips in a thin hard line.

Miranda sensed that the battle between the two men had begun and that nothing she could say or do would prevent it. Even so, as they sat down to the salad, she made an attempt to launch the conversation on a safe subject, the natural beauties of Killarney.

Brian responded with a strained smile, but Frazier introduced a question of his own.

"Walter Royce is taking me fishing for salmon tomorrow in what I understand is your stream, O'Bannon. I can't offer you a series of lectures or the prospect of a book in exchange. Is there any other way I can pay you for the privilege?"

Shocked, Miranda cried, "Frazier! That's an insult."

"Not at all," he answered smoothly. "Brian is a man of the world, even though he's a poet—or perhaps especially because he's a poet, since people who live by their wits instead of work have to resort to very worldly stratagems to get by."

Miranda drew her breath in with a sharp hiss. She started to protest against this further insult, then closed her mouth firmly. Her father's outrageous behavior was like the sputtering end of a string of firecrackers that led somewhere familiar, and she needed time to figure out where.

An urbanely smiling Brian deflected Frazier's contempt. "The privilege will be mine, sir," he said, "to have the opportunity of accommodating an eminent American scientist."

Although Frazier accepted the compliment with only a curt nod, Miranda could see that he was pleased. He sat a little straighter in his chair and set his handsome profile in a pose that reminded Miranda of the epithets *pompous, vain,* and *egotistical* applied to Frazier Dunn by various scientific colleagues who hadn't known she was the man's daughter.

In the brief silence that followed, Miranda recaptured the scene of which this was an imperfect repetition. It had taken place in her apartment in New York on one of Craig's weekends with her.

Miranda had invited her father to dinner, and the three of them were sitting at the table having dessert and coffee. Miranda had told her father that because their commuter marriage wasn't working out, she had decided to leave her job in Manhattan and go to Minneapolis to live with Craig there. Frazier had belittled the idea so effectively, including in his disparagement Craig's scientific ability, that Miranda had given up the idea. Eventually, her marriage had collapsed, and that, Miranda now thought with a raised eyebrow, might well have been Frazier's motive, albeit an unconscious one.

As she removed the salad plates and served the fish course, Miranda listened to the conversation of the two

men. Frazier was expounding on his contributions to
science, on the recognition he had already received from
colleagues, and the important work that still lay ahead
of him. "But of course one would have to be a scientist,"
Frazier said, bringing his recital to an end, "to understand
fully the scope of my work."

But of course one would have to be a scientist—how
blind I've been not to have seen it before, Miranda thought.
He's always needed acclaim; but with the cheers getting
fewer as he ages and his creative years in science slip
away, he needs it more than ever. And for this acclaim
to be valid, it can't come from just anybody, but has to
be from someone who really understands. Mom doesn't
know anything about science and couldn't care less. But
a daughter who's been brought up to be a scientist by a
doting father—especially an unmarried daughter whose
affections aren't divided—ah! what a hero-worshiper she
makes.

A tremendous feeling of freedom swept over Miranda,
like a wave carrying beach debris out to sea and leaving
everything clean behind it. She glanced at Brian, noting
the quiet attention he was paying her father, and realized
it had all been deliberate on Brian's part. Using his imagination and intuitive understanding of people, he had
gently exposed Frazier to Miranda, showing her he was
less the hero than she had thought and that the principles
he had laid down for her weren't always true. Miranda
realized now that subconsciously she had always mea-
sured the men she loved against this paternal model and
found them wanting. The model had proved to be made
of clay; but even if it hadn't, the act of measuring, evaluating, judging, put restrictions on love that didn't belong
there. Love was free or it wasn't love.

Brian caught her looking at him and gave her a quiet
smile.

Miranda then transferred her gaze to her father. "Dad,"

she said firmly, "I have something important to tell you."

Frazier's dark eyebrows shot up in a supercilious arc and his mouth tightened with disapproval at her use of a term he had once damned as sentimental.

Ignoring his look, Miranda reached across the table and took Brian's hand in hers. "Brian has asked me to marry him, Dad, and I'm accepting now. I'm going to be Miranda Dunn-O'Bannon, as I was once Miranda Dunn-Jones. Only, this time I'll never be Miranda Dunn again. I'm also going to collaborate with Brian on the book I told you about. As for the fellowship—I'll decide about that in my own good time." Suddenly struck by a horrible thought, Miranda searched Brian's face anxiously for his reaction. "You do still want to marry me, don't you?"

His clear eyes held hers for a long moment. "More than ever—if that's possible."

"You're making another mistake, Miranda," Frazier said. "I don't understand why you're always attracted to men who want to use you. It's almost as though you doubted your ability to hold a man any other way."

Miranda felt Brian's hand tighten on hers. His eyes went cold and hard, but before he could say anything, Miranda laughed with all the gusto and freedom she now felt. "Dad, you're impossible. Brian doesn't want to *use* me. He *loves* me."

"You've got a lot of faith, Miranda," her father said dryly.

"In Brian?" Miranda looked at her lover tenderly and squeezed his hand. "You bet!"

Frazier pushed his chair back and prepared to get up. "Well, your mother will be glad you're getting married again."

Miranda released her hand from Brian's grasp and placed it over her father's hand. "So will you be, Dad."

"I hope so," Frazier answered heavily. He rose and

looked down at her with grudging admiration. "I'll say one thing for you—you may have picked the wrong man again, but this time you're fighting for him." He reached across the table to where Brian had also risen and shook his hand. "No hard feelings, I trust. I hope your book makes lots of money."

"I hope so, too, sir, as I've already earmarked part of the royalties for poetry therapy."

"What's that?" Frazier asked suspiciously.

"It's a program that uses poetry as therapy for the mentally ill. I learned about it when I once gave a reading in a mental hospital in Dublin. My audience ranged from staff psychiatrists to schizophrenic patients. When I finished reading one poem, a woman patient began talking in an incomprehensible deluge of words. We couldn't understand what she was saying, but what was happening to her was important. The poem seemingly had opened up something inside her; it had helped her 'get it out,' so to speak.

"Literature is universal. When a patient who thought his inner pain was unexplainable hears another human being describe a similar pain in a poem or song, he apparently feels rescued from a terrible isolation. I've been told that as a result of joining a group where poems are read aloud, discussed, or written, psychotically mute patients have started to talk, hostile ones have become calm, and despairing ones have acquired hope. There is no doubt in my mind that poetry is a healer, and I plan to support my belief by providing at least some funds for the program."

Miranda's eyes glowed with pride. This was probably what Walter had wanted to tell her about Brian. It was a complete vindication of Brian's motives—in Frazier's eyes; *she* hadn't needed this proof, Miranda thought joyfully. She had aligned herself on Brian's side and pledged herself to him before she knew about his altruistic intentions. Love had given her the faith she needed.

Frazier received Brian's explanation with a noncommittal "humph" and turned to Miranda. "I hope you'll decide to take that fellowship," he said sternly. "Naturally, your mother and I will come to your wedding, and of course you'll let us know where you intend to live."

"Do you have to go, Dad? There's still coffee and dessert to come."

"I'm sorry, but I forgot that one of the men at Biochem wanted to see me. Your lunch was delicious, Miranda. I'm sorry I can't stay for all of it, but I'll be back later in the afternoon." He turned to Brian. His face expressionless and his tone level, he said only, "Good-bye for now, O'Bannon."

Brian bowed slightly, and Frazier stalked out.

Brian leaned over Miranda and pulled her gently to her feet, folding her in his arms. "Don't feel bad, *macushla*. He's upset now, but he'll come round."

She raised her face to his and looked candidly in his eyes. "That's the funny part. I don't want to see him hurt or to hurt him, but I can't feel bad because I feel so marvelously free—free of always wondering what he'd think, whether he would approve, of trying to meet his standards and knowing I never can."

Brian nodded. "I understand. He's free now, too. He doesn't have to be a hero any longer." He wrapped her closer to him and ran his lips over her hair in a string of gentle kisses. "And when the kids start coming, believe me, he'll be happy as Larry."

"Who's Larry?" Miranda asked.

Brian grinned. "Nobody knows who Larry was or why he was so happy." His voice dropped to a husky whisper. "All I know is, he couldn't have been as happy as I am at this moment." His lips sought hers in a long, fulfilling kiss.

"Were you surprised when I said I was going to marry you?"

"Not at all. Sure and haven't I been saying the exact same thing from the first day I met you?" He pushed her hair off her face now with his lips, repeatedly brushing her skin in tantalizing strokes that made her want him at that very moment.

But now was not the time, and Miranda pulled away slightly. "How about dessert and coffee?" she asked.

"That depends on what's for dessert." He reached for her again, his hands covering her breasts and curving around her slim sides.

Miranda pushed his hands away. "It's a sponge cake I made myself, and you can wipe that evil grin off your face."

Brian dropped his hands and sat down, a rueful look in his eyes. "I'm probably the only man who ever sublimated with sponge cake." When Miranda had sat down opposite him, he asked, "What's this fellowship your dad mentioned? You haven't told me anything about it."

"It's for two years of work and study at the Wolcott Research Institute in New York."

"Is it a good opportunity?" Brian asked softly.

"The best."

"Then you'll be leaving—when?"

"I've decided not to take it, Brian. I've got a good job here. I'm doing important research and learning a lot. And if I stay, we won't have to separate." Miranda reached for Brian's hand across the table.

He took it, but in an absentminded way that made Miranda wonder. "Frazier seemed to think you should take the fellowship."

"My father's the scientific equivalent of a Hollywood stage mother," Miranda said dryly. Her voice becoming earnest and tight, she continued, "I know what separation can do to a marriage, Brian. I couldn't endure being apart from you."

"The world needs dedicated scientists like you, Miranda. You might well consider it your duty to accept the fellowship. And you don't have to make a choice."

"What do you mean?"

"I could no more stand a commuter marriage than you could. Sure and I'd never know which bed I was sleeping in," he added with a smile. "I'll go to New York with you. A poet can write anywhere. My publisher is in New York. And I've enough of a reputation now, so I can always teach at one of your universities."

"You would do that—for me?" Miranda said.

"It's not the kind of offer I go around making to every beautiful woman I meet."

"Then I'll be able to have my cake and eat it too," Miranda said thoughtfully.

"Always the best arrangement, in my opinion." Brian gave her the quick sidelong smile that never failed to gladden her heart. "Is that ban on my celebrating our love still in effect?"

Miranda beamed and shook her head. "You can shout it from the rooftops if you want to."

Chapter Fourteen

BUT IT WAS not from the rooftops that Miranda heard it. A few days later, as she was preparing bacterial cultures to be centrifuged, a voice came over the plant loudspeaker which was normally used only for fire drills or very important announcements. The voice wasn't Brian's, but the poem was. Miranda turned scarlet and wished she could sink out of sight as a secretary in Administration, her voice bubbling with laughter, introduced Brian O'Bannon's "September Ode" dedicated to Miranda Dunn and then read an unmistakable love poem.

The poem was discreet, light, and amusing—and it made everyone's day. Her colleagues kidded her. Walter Royce came out of his office, beaming. Janet called a short while later to say that Miranda and Brian could use the Royces' house for the wedding reception. When Miranda finally escaped to the cafeteria, she had to run a gauntlet of grins before she could slink to a rear table with a hastily snatched dish of red Jell-O and cottage cheese, which she abhorred.

By afternoon, Miranda and her colleagues were again absorbed in their work, the amusing incident pushed to the back of their minds. But as Miranda buckled her raincoat around her at the end of the day, her thoughts reverted to the poem and she repeated to herself with secret pleasure the words Brian had written to her. Day-dreaming a little about her happiness—present and future—Miranda stepped out the front door and stopped short.

Groups of employees were scattered about on the green lawn, looking up into the sky at a small plane pulling a plume of smoke across rapidly darkening clouds. Staring straight upward and concentrating, Miranda could make out the word BROVESANDA. But what did it mean? Wrinkling her nose in puzzlement, she asked Sheila, "Is it an ad for a new product?"

The secretary's eyes were dancing as she said, "Sure and some of the letters got blown away by the wind before you came out. But the writing said, 'Brian loves Miranda,' and it looked just beautiful up there in the sky."

"I'll bet," Miranda muttered to herself. She managed to stammer a "Thanks, Sheila," then closed her eyes in utter disbelief of what was happening. Maybe when she opened them again, the crowd would have dispersed to their various pushbikes and motorbikes, caravans and cars and be on their way home.

But no, Biochem looked like nothing so much as a movie set for an extravaganza, with hundreds of extras cued to smile on command as soon as the leading lady appeared on the lawn. *"Forget the plot," the director told them. "Just smile, grin, smirk, twinkle, simper, ogle, leer, and beam. Keep it up. She's walking toward you now. Don't stop! Don't stop! Smile, dammit, smile! And when she gets into her car, burst into wild applause. That's it! Terrific! Cut! Very good, all you extras. Eight o'clock tomorrow sharp! Our scriptwriter, Brian O'Bannon, will have another big scene for you."*

"I've got to put a stop to this," Miranda said aloud to herself as she threw her car in gear. "I should never have told him he could celebrate our love. He's wild and crazy and"—her voice softened as certain images came before her mind's eye—"wonderful and"—she relaxed against the seat—"what Aunt Janet said he was, so why don't I drive to his cabin right now and suggest he go private with our love instead of public?"

But Brian's cabin was locked, with no key to be found and no way to get in. Disappointed, Miranda wandered a short way along the salmon stream; but it was much too dark for fishing and she recalled that Brian's motorbike was missing from the front of the cabin, so she went home to supper and bed and a new scientific journal.

The next day, the loudspeaker was silent and the skies were empty. Work took precedence over all until a giggling, pink-cheeked Jill brought the cage of lab mice Miranda had requested. A red paper heart with an entwined B. O'B. and M. D. printed on it hung from each furry neck.

"Jill!" Miranda said sharply. "This violates the animal-care regulations. You really shouldn't have done it. Please take the signs off."

"I'm sorry, miss," the young woman said in a brogue to match Sheila's. "It was only a joke. It won't really hurt them. And Mr. O'Bannon seemed so . . ."

"I know," Miranda said wearily. "You don't have to tell me. So charming and persuasive."

Jill bent her head over the cage, her face beet-red as she exploded in mirth. "So much in love, I was going to say."

Miranda rolled her eyes upward. Where *was* the man? She had to find him and stop him before he prevented her from getting any work done at all. Bending over the cage to help Jill, she said, "When did you last see Mr. O'Bannon? It must have been today."

"It was midday, miss—just before I went to lunch."

"Did he say where he was going?" Miranda asked casually.

Jill looked at her with clear-eyed innocence. "He said something about getting a little exercise by helping the lads pour the cement for that parking lot they're forever putting in and taking out."

Miranda nodded grimly and looked at her watch. "In other words, he told you he'd be there now."

"That's true." Jill managed to get insincere guilt, amusement, and curiosity into her expression all at the same time. "Are you going out to him, then?"

"You can put the mice away, Jill," Miranda said grandly. "I won't be needing them today."

"Yes, miss." Jill bent her head over the cage again, but too late to hide her smile.

Miranda strode to the coat rack and hung up her lab coat. She lifted her raincoat off the hook and scrambled into it as she hurried to the back door. The sun had broken through, and the day was Indian-summer warm. The men mixing and pouring cement had stripped to the waist and Brian was among them, helping a slight, very pale young man carry bags of cement. Sweat shone on Brian's bare shoulders and glistened in the tight, curly pelt on his chest.

Miranda's heart turned over when she saw him. Secure in the knowledge that he didn't know she was there, she watched him a few minutes longer, relishing the strength of his muscular arms, the skill with which he handled the heavy bags of cement, and his easy camaraderie with the workmen. Then he spotted her, and the sight of his devil-may-care grin reminded Miranda what she had come out for.

Under the frankly interested gaze of the men, who

leaned on their shovels to watch, Brian made his way to her and bent his head for a kiss. Her quick averting of her lips intensified public interest, and any man who had been working now stopped.

"I don't want any more, Brian," Miranda said firmly. "No more loudspeaker poems, no more love words in the sky, no more Valentine's Day lab mice. You're disrupting science."

"Sure, *macushla,* you know I'd never do that—not when science means so much to you. I just couldn't help myself. I wanted the whole world to know how I feel about you."

"It does," Miranda said wryly. "People point me out in the cafeteria line; the lab techs have gotten up a pool on our wedding date; and Janet wants to have the reception in her house..."

She was going to say more, but Brian interrupted her. "Janet's planning something very posh. Your father's returning from Geneva for it, and your mother's coming from the States. And Barbara Evans and *her* fiancé are coming—that fellow who has trouble with numbers—and..."

This time it was Miranda's turn to interrupt. "You've got it all planned among you, haven't you? Only it's not a surprise birthday party. It's a wedding—*my* wedding—and I'd like to have something to say about it. I didn't even know my best friend was engaged." Miranda's voice had risen with plaintive indignation. She had forgotten where she was and that she had an audience.

A few deep baritones saying, "That's right," "She's right, you know," "Let the lass plan her own wedding," reminded her.

"Oh, no," she murmured. "Not again. Isn't there any such thing as privacy in this place?"

Putting his half-naked body between Miranda and the men, Brian blocked her from their view. "I know a place where we can be alone," he said softly.

Miranda stared at the manly fuzz on his chest and his taut, sun-browned stomach and knew that her anger was turning into something else. Brian moved closer, and the scent of his sweat was an aphrodisiac. She felt that part of her that said no before it said yes—that looked for rules, that sought out structure in everything—unraveling. She was becoming warm and lax and excited inside.

"No one goes there at this time of year—to the fairy isle of Innisfallen. Do you remember how it was with us there, *macushla?*" Brian put one hand up on the wall of the building, alongside her. A slight flection of his knees caused their torsos to touch.

Weak with desire for him, Miranda nevertheless pressed the small of her back against the smooth concrete of the building. Simultaneously, she put the flat of her palm against Brian's hard stomach to ward him off. However, the feel of his warm, solid flesh was so enticing that she yielded to the temptation of leaving her hand there, tucked just inside the belt of his jeans. "Brian," she said breathlessly, "I can't go off with you every time you want me to. I might lose my job."

"You won't, I assure you."

It was absurd, but she couldn't help herself. "You didn't give Walter so many salmon for me, did you?"

He bent his head to her again and whispered, "There aren't enough salmon in my salmon stream to pay for you, *macushla.*" Then, straightening up, he spoke in his usual baritone, "Are you coming or aren't you?"

"Go with him, lass," came a voice from the crowd.

Another, less polite—possibly the foreman—yelled, "Go along, the two of yez, and let us get our work done, will ye."

With her eyes closed and through clenched teeth, Miranda said, "I'm going, Brian. I'm getting out of here right now."

"Will you meet me in front and go with me to Innisfallen, then?" he whispered.

"Yes," she hissed. "Anything to get off the stage."

He took the wheel of her car, as usual. Looking at him, a checkered shirt buttoned low on his virile chest, the sleeves rolled up to his biceps, Miranda felt her blood race like quicksilver in her veins. She was desirous of what was to come but had misgivings, too. "Tourists *do* visit Killarney in the fall," she said. "And Innisfallen *is* popular."

"There are no boatmen left to take them, and I don't think it's going to be a good day for swimming."

Following his lead, Miranda looked upward through the windshield. Great silver-edged gray schooners bellied their way across the sky. "I can't believe it," she said with a gasp. "It was sunny only a few minutes ago."

"That's Killarney for you. If you don't like the weather, just wait a bit."

"Will it be safe on the lake?"

Brian nodded. "There's no real wind. It'll rain some, then let up." He glanced sideways at her with a secret little smile. "The way it did before."

Miranda looked straight ahead, but her smile matched his. "Will the boat still be there?"

Brian rolled his eyes and nodded in answer.

"You *know* it's there! You *planned* all this! You're positively Machiavellian!"

Brian shook his head. "The name's O'Bannon. Mac Vellian's from another county altogether."

Miranda groaned, and Brian's face split in a huge, happy grin.

The rowboat was still where they had left it—in the tall grass bordering the lake. As they shoved off from shore and headed out on the water, Miranda sensed again the enchantment of the place—the lonely, still lake and the dark, misty islands in its center, and in the distance, the purple mountains, their heads turbaned in gray clouds.

When the rain came, it was a gentle, warm drizzle that seemed scarcely to wet them. Miranda spread her raincoat across both their laps, then held her face up to feel the moisture on her skin. "It's as though every-thing—the sky, the lake, the air—were water," she said in a tone of wonder, "and we're just floating through it, and if we keep going, we'll pass right through into the O'Donoghue's mountain and not come out for seven years."

"Or seventy. There's no time in fairyland."

"Janet would be disappointed—no wedding recep-tion," Miranda mused.

"But Walter could have all the salmon in my stream."

"My father would scold, 'This is a terrible setback to your career, Miranda. You'll never be able to catch up after seventy years.'"

"At least Colin won't be able to transpose *seventy-seven*."

"But Barbara would say, 'That's really living to-gether!—shut up in a mountain for seventy years.'"

They both laughed, then were silent as Brian tied up the boat at the landing stage and helped Miranda out. Silently, hand in hand, they walked through the lush, rain-shiny groves of Innisfallen.

"It's so lovely, Brian, its beauty so much a part of our happiness, that I can hardly bear it," Miranda said. "Now *I* want to celebrate our love. What's a wedding song called again?"

"An epithalamium," Brian supplied readily.

Miranda laughed. "I'll bet you expected me to say epithelium." She fell silent again, thinking. Then, dis-appointed, she complained, "I don't know how to begin my poem."

"Begin with what you see," Brian said quietly.

Slowly, haltingly, like someone learning a new language, Miranda said, "If you come my way, I will give you leaves shaped like long cups to drink from/and bird choirs fretful as children at bedtime to hear./I'll lie with you on the soft green-haired turf/and be your lover for seven and seventy years. If you come my way." She laughed, embarrassed. "That's the best I can do. I'm still better at naming plants than writing poetry about them."

Husky-voiced, Brian said, "Don't apologize. It's a beautiful poem."

They had reached the oak glen where they first consummated their love. Feverishly, they sought each other's closeness. Brian wrapped his arms around Miranda and pulled her tight to him. His mouth covered hers in ravenous kisses that moved restlessly over her face and hair and neck. "I love you so much," he whispered. "You are the other I have been waiting for all my life, my partner, my joy."

He spread the raincoat for her and eased her gently down onto it. She reached her arms up for him as, kneeling, he undressed her. His own clothes came next. The sibilant rustle of the leaves in the rain mingled with his words of love.

Looking down at her breasts reverently, Brian murmured, "They're lovely and full as white-sailed ships when the wind is behind them." Lowering his lips to the smooth, silky flesh, he exhaled his warm breath over each in turn, raising goose pimples of delight on her flesh and bringing her nipples to a throbbing tautness. He passed the stubble of his cheek across each pink meringue peak so that his lips would feel the softer and sweeter to Miranda when he closed them around each one. His mouth descended then to her small, hard belly, the start of an exciting trail of open, moist kisses that led downward to the quivering heart of her longing.

Miranda stretched under his caresses, eager to expose

all of herself to his delectable kisses. She threaded her
hands through his damp hair and moaned with joy as he
continued to pleasure her. She thought that, coupled with
the knowledge they now had of each other—of what
delighted and what thrilled—was the eternal mystery of
the other person, the realization that if they lived together
for seventy-seven years, there would always still be that
x factor to maintain their interest. Sameness would be
no threat. They would never tire of each other.

Masterfully, Brian raised his lean body and entered
her. In that sudden fullness, that titanic coming together,
Miranda felt a cosmic rapture. She was fused with the
man she loved in a timeless rhythm bound up with
the turning wheel of the seasons, with the rivers that
rushed to the sea and the clouds that gave the rain and
drew it up into the sky again.

Their eyes met, and his smiled at her. "I love you,
macushla," he said joyously.

"And I love you, Brian," she answered, her voice
vibrant with emotion.

He continued to whisper to her—sweet words, crazy
words, and words she had never heard before. Were they
Irish or had he made them up? Whatever...they made
her laugh and aroused her and went with her from peak
to ever-higher peak of a glorious wave-tossed sea. Finally, they lay, spent and sated, clasping each other like
survivors cast up on some far-off sands.

"What were you saying to me, Brian?" Miranda asked
when she could talk again.

"It was a language I made up for the occasion, *macushla*, thinking the everyday words not good enough."

Miranda stretched languorously. "And they aren't,
darling, believe me. Could you do it again?"

"Make up more words?"

Miranda laughed gaily at him, and Brian, catching
on, grinned. Then his expression became serious. "We'd

best go back, *macushla*. It's beginning to rain in earnest."

She wound her arms around his waist. "Sure it's only the Killarney mist. It'll clear up soon."

"The rain's coming in on us, Miranda," he said a little sharply. "We're getting wet."

"Rain's necessary for life—for plants and crops and to refill streams," Miranda murmured, feathering her hands over his thighs. She raised her head and put her lips to his bare shoulder. "Don't worry, darling," she continued huskily. "I'll warm you."

Brian chuckled. "Miranda, are you blarneying me?"

"Only just a little," she whispered, "to get my own way and to refute the ugly rumor that poets do it with words."

Brian took her in his arms. "I thought I had already scotched that rumor."

"Science demands *so* much proof." Miranda sighed with simulated resignation as she ran her hands with exquisite delight down his muscular, smooth-skinned back.

"Sure and it's a sweet martyrdom your science exacts," Brian answered.

Together, then, they began again the passionate exploration that leads to ecstatic discovery of the Self and the beloved Other.

Second Chance at Love ®

____ 06650-8 **ON WINGS OF MAGIC #62** Susanna Collins $1.75
____ 06693-1 **TARNISHED RAINBOW #82** Jocelyn Day $1.75
____ 06695-8 **LOVER IN BLUE #84** Aimée Duvall $1.75
____ 06851-9 **A MAN'S PERSUASION #89** Katherine Granger $1.75
____ 06858-6 **BREATHLESS DAWN #94** Susanna Collins $1.75
____ 06863-2 **THE FORGOTTEN BRIDE #99** Lillian Marsh $1.75
____ 06864-0 **A PROMISE TO CHERISH #100** LaVyrle Spencer $1.75
____ 06867-5 **ENTHRALLED #103** Ann Cristy $1.75
____ 06870-5 **RELENTLESS DESIRE #106** Sandra Brown $1.75
____ 06874-8 **TAKEN BY STORM #110** Kay Robbins $1.75
____ 07200-1 **A LASTING TREASURE #112** Cally Hughes
____ 07203-6 **COME WINTER'S END #115** Claire Evans
____ 07212-5 **SONG FOR A LIFETIME #124** Mary Haskell
____ 07213-3 **HIDDEN DREAMS #125** Johanna Phillips
____ 07214-1 **LONGING UNVEILED #126** Meredith Kingston
____ 07215-X **JADE TIDE #127** Jena Hunt
____ 07216-8 **THE MARRYING KIND #128** Jocelyn Day
____ 07217-6 **CONQUERING EMBRACE #129** Ariel Tierney
____ 07218-4 **ELUSIVE DAWN #130** Kay Robbins
____ 07219-2 **ON WINGS OF PASSION #131** Beth Brookes
____ 07220-6 **WITH NO REGRETS #132** Nuria Wood
____ 07221-4 **CHERISHED MOMENTS #133** Sarah Ashley
____ 07222-2 **PARISIAN NIGHTS #134** Susanna Collins
____ 07223-0 **GOLDEN ILLUSIONS #135** Sarah Crewe
____ 07224-9 **ENTWINED DESTINIES #136** Rachel Wayne
____ 07225-7 **TEMPTATION'S KISS #137** Sandra Brown
____ 07226-5 **SOUTHERN PLEASURES #138** Daisy Logan
____ 07227-3 **FORBIDDEN MELODY #139** Nicola Andrews
____ 07228-1 **INNOCENT SEDUCTION #140** Cally Hughes
____ 07229-X **SEASON OF DESIRE #141** Jan Mathews
____ 07230-3 **HEARTS DIVIDED #142** Francine Rivers
____ 07231-1 **A SPLENDID OBSESSION #143** Francesca Sinclaire
____ 07232-X **REACH FOR TOMORROW #144** Mary Haskell
____ 07233-8 **CLAIMED BY RAPTURE #145** Marie Charles
____ 07234-6 **A TASTE FOR LOVING #146** Frances Davies
____ 07235-4 **PROUD POSSESSION #147** Jena Hunt
____ 07236-2 **SILKEN TREMORS #148** Sybil LeGrand
____ 07237-0 **A DARING PROPOSITION #149** Jeanne Grant
____ 07238-9 **ISLAND FIRES #150** Jocelyn Day
____ 07239-7 **MOONLIGHT ON THE BAY #151** Maggie Peck
____ 07240-0 **ONCE MORE WITH FEELING #152** Melinda Harris
____ 07241-9 **INTIMATE SCOUNDRELS #153** Cathy Thacker
____ 07242-7 **STRANGER IN PARADISE #154** Laurel Blake
____ 07243-5 **KISSED BY MAGIC #155** Kay Robbins
____ 07244-3 **LOVESTRUCK #156** Margot Leslie

All of the above titles are $1.95 per copy except where noted

SK-41a

All of the above titles are $1.95
Prices may be slightly higher in Canada.

Available at your local bookstore or return this form to:

 SECOND CHANCE AT LOVE
Book Mailing Service
P.O. Box 690, Rockville Centre, NY 11571

Please send me the titles checked above. I enclose _____. Include 75¢ for postage and handling if one book is ordered; 25¢ per book for two or more not to exceed $1.75. California, Illinois, New York and Tennessee residents please add sales tax.

NAME _____

ADDRESS _____

CITY _____ STATE/ZIP _____
(allow six weeks for delivery)   SK-41b

NEW FROM THE PUBLISHERS OF *SECOND CHANCE AT LOVE!*

To Have and to Hold

___	**THE TESTIMONY #1** Robin James	06928-0
___	**A TASTE OF HEAVEN #2** Jennifer Rose	06929-9
___	**TREAD SOFTLY #3** Ann Cristy	06930-2
___	**THEY SAID IT WOULDN'T LAST #4** Elaine Tucker	06931-0
___	**GILDED SPRING #5** Jenny Bates	06932-9
___	**LEGAL AND TENDER #6** Candice Adams	06933-7
___	**THE FAMILY PLAN #7** Nuria Wood	06934-5
___	**HOLD FAST 'TIL DAWN #8** Mary Haskell	06935-3
___	**HEART FULL OF RAINBOWS #9** Melanie Randolph	06936-1
___	**I KNOW MY LOVE #10** Vivian Connolly	06937-X
___	**KEYS TO THE HEART #11** Jennifer Rose	06938-8
___	**STRANGE BEDFELLOWS #12** Elaine Tucker	06939-6
___	**MOMENTS TO SHARE #13** Katharine Granger	06940-X
___	**SUNBURST #14** Jeanne Grant	06941-8
___	**WHATEVER IT TAKES #15** Cally Hughes	06942-6
___	**LADY LAUGHING EYES #16** Lee Damon	06943-4
___	**ALL THAT GLITTERS #17** Mary Haskell	06944-2
___	**PLAYING FOR KEEPS #18** Elissa Curry	06945-0
___	**PASSION'S GLOW #19** Marilyn Brian	06946-9
___	**BETWEEN THE SHEETS #20** Tricia Adams	06947-7
___	**MOONLIGHT AND MAGNOLIAS #21** Vivian Connolly	06948-5
___	**A DELICATE BALANCE #22** Kate Wellington	06949-3
___	**KISS ME, CAIT #23** Elissa Curry	07825-5
___	**HOMECOMING #24** Ann Cristy	07826-3
___	**TREASURE TO SHARE #25** Cally Hughes	07827-1

All Titles are $1.95

Prices may be slightly higher in Canada.

Available at your local bookstore or return this form to:

SECOND CHANCE AT LOVE
Book Mailing Service
P.O. Box 690, Rockville Centre, NY 11571

Please send me the titles checked above. I enclose _____ Include 75¢ for postage and handling if one book is ordered; 25¢ per book for two or more not to exceed $1.75. California, Illinois, New York and Tennessee residents please add sales tax.

NAME_____

ADDRESS_____

CITY_____ STATE/ZIP_____
(allow six weeks for delivery)   **THTH #67**

HERE'S WHAT READERS ARE SAYING ABOUT

Second Chance at Love ®

"I think your books are great. I love to read them
as does my family."
— P. S., Milford, MA*

"Your books are some of the best romances
I've read."
— M. B., Zeeland, MI*

"SECOND CHANCE AT LOVE is my favorite line
of romance novels."
— L. B., Springfield, VA*

"I think SECOND CHANCE AT LOVE books are
terrific. I married my 'Second Chance' over
15 years ago. I truly believe love is lovelier
the second time around!"
— P. P., Houston, TX*

"I enjoy your books tremendously."
— I. S., Bayonne, NJ*

"I love your books and read them all the time.
Keep them coming—they're just great."
— G. L., Brookfield, CT*

"SECOND CHANCE AT LOVE books are
definitely the best!"
— D. P., Wabash, IN*

*Name and address available upon request